Summer 1990

A Young Adult Novel

by

FIRYAL ALSHALABI

Aunt Strawberry Books
Boulder, Colorado

Cover design by Bob Schram/Bookends
Cover illustration by Joe Howard

Library of Congress Catalog Card Number: 99-94611

Summary: Separated from her family by the Iraqi invasion of Kuwait, spoiled thirteen year old Danah, stealthily returns to say "sorry" to her parents and help liberate her country.
1-Kuwait--fiction 2-Gulf War--fiction 3-Adolescence
ISBN 978-09669988-0-4

First Printing January 1999
Printed in the United States of America

Aunt Strawberry Books
P.O. Box 819
Boulder, CO 80306-0819

Dedication

*I dedicate this book to **Mohammed Jasem Kamal,** who was my student in Kuwait before the invasion. He was captured by the Iraqis on Saturday the 18th of August 1990 and was never heard from since. I look forward to the day when Mohammed and more than 600 other POW's return home safely to their families and friends.*

Books By Firyal Alshalabi

Zarazir (A Kuwaiti Folktale)

Grandpa Saleh and Pearl Diving

Grandmother Dalal

Ahmed's Alphabet Book

Summer 1990

Acknowledgements

A heartfelt gratitude to Sam Dreksler whose faith in my writing kept me going. His editing, encouragement and support brought this work and many others to life. Thank you Sam, I'm forever indebted.

I would also like to thank David Ambroson who sparked the idea for this novel during the Virginia Westerberg Children's Literature Conference. Thank you David, that was so brilliant of you.

I wish to thank Professor Ruth Cline, my teacher and friend, whose guidance and friendship have always been invaluable and greatly appreciated. Thank you Ruth, you've been an inspiration to me and your students.

A big thank you to Barbara Ciletti who pushed me forward every time I stumbled backward during the work on this project. Thank you Barbara, you're an angel.

Many thanks and gratitude to the people at Kuwait Information Center, in Washington, D.C., for their generous support. I'd like to especially mention Mr. Tareq Al-Mezrem and Mr. Mohammed Al-Bdah for their cooperation and assistance. Thank you all very much, without your help and support this book would not have materialized.

Definitions Of Arabic Words Used In The Book:

Abaya:	A traditional black cloak worn by some Kuwaiti women over the head to cover clothes upon leaving dwelling.
Allah:	The Arabic word for God
Alhamdu Lillah:	Praise be to God.
Bu:	'The father of'. Usually followed by the first name of the eldest son.
Burga':	A face cover worn by Bedouin women, made of black cotton, with two narrow slits for the eyes.
Danah:	A popular female name in Kuwait based on 'Eddanah', an old name for a large pearl. Pronounced: Dah nah
Dishdasha:	A traditional long garment with long sleeves worn by men. It is usually made of light white fabric in summer, and dark colored wool in winter.
Ghitra:	A traditional head cover made of a square white light fabric. In winter it is usually made of a thicker white and red material.
In Sha' Allah:	If God wills.
Mahbi:	Kuwaiti for: I don't want to.
Om:	'The mother of'. Usually followed by the first name of the eldest son.
Ogal:	A double circlet of black twisted wool worn by men on top of the head to hold the ghitra in place.
Wallah:	I swear to God.
Yuba:	Kuwaiti dialect for 'Dad'.
Yumma:	Kuwaiti dialect for 'Mom'.
Zain:	Kuwaiti for: all right.

Summer 1990

CHAPTER ONE

July 1, 1990

*D*ANAH WAS NOT HAPPY. Summer vacation had already started and she should be having fun, but Kuwait was just too hot to do anything outdoors. So she stayed in bed in her air-conditioned room and read all morning.

In the afternoon, she went upstairs to see what her sister Amani was doing. Perhaps they'd do something fun together. But Amani was posing in front of the long closet mirror, trying on her new ankle length dress for the tea party that night.

The emerald gown made Amani's big hazel eyes look green. The color complemented her silky brown hair. She looked so beautiful.

'Bedr el bedoor', her father had always called Amani, the moon of all moons. That was what his grandmother, the bedouin beauty, had been called. There was even a bedouin poem written about her.

"What about me?" Danah would say, feeling left out, every time her father told the story of Bedr el bedoor.

"You are ed Danah, the pearl of all pearls," he would answer.

"Danah!" Amani snapped, slipping out of the evening gown. "Answer the phone! Can't you help just a little?" She stretched for the bath robe hanging behind the door.

"Ooof!" Danah complained. "Why? Did someone tell you I'm your receptionist?"

Still, she reached for the phone on the night table, and knocked it down to the floor. Giggling, she picked up the receiver. "Aloo?" she listened for a second, then handed it to Amani. "It's Auntie Ibtisam, your future mother-in-law."

Amani took the phone and covered the mouth piece with her hand, irritation clear all over her delicate features. "Danah, get out of my room."

"Mahbi, I don't want to!" Danah said, stomping her bare feet into the carpet. She stared defiantly at Amani, but inched backward to the door. Just because she was only thirteen and Amani was twenty, didn't mean she could boss her around.

"Ahlan Khaltie, hello auntie," Amani said amiably. She sat on the edge of her bed, and combed her waist-long hair. "No, we just finished having lunch."

"Ahlan Khaltie," Danah mimicked Amani. She squinted her eyes and shook her head. "We just finished having lunch." Then she stuck her tongue out and scooted out the door, skipping down the winding staircase to the first floor.

A strong fragrance of frankincense permeated the living room. Danah covered her nose with her hand. Frankincense reminded her of weddings. She hated weddings. That was probably what her parents were discussing when she entered the room because they stopped talking when they saw her. Bimla, the Indian maid, sprinkled rose water around the room from a pear-shaped brass sprinkler. With her other hand she held a brass incense burner, she placed them both on the coffee table, and left the room.

Danah threw herself on the couch facing her parents.

"Look at her," her father said smiling, showing the dimples he must have inherited from Bedr el bedoor himself. "Doesn't she look more and more like her brother Aziz?"

Her mother's long dark face remained serious. "She's almost as tall as he is."

"Ooof!" Danah protested. "Just because I wear my hair short doesn't mean I look like a boy!"

"Lower your voice," her father said firmly, though his face did not show anger. He wore a gleaming white dishdasha, and his ogal and ghitra were already in place over his head, a sign he was going out soon. "Did you do your afternoon prayers?" he asked.

"Yes, why do you have to ask?" She turned toward her mother and said, "Yumma, take me to the bookstore."

"We just took you to the bookstore last week, when your summer vacation began."

Danah waited for the grandfather clock in the corner of the room to finish striking four-thirty. "I read all the books I bought, wallah. I have nothing else to do. By the way, Yuba," she addressed her father. "You didn't give me my monthly allowance yet."

Her father sighed deeply before he pulled out his wallet from the front pocket of his dishdasha. He took out several five dinar bills and handed them to Danah.

"What else, ha?" her mother asked, frowning, the fine lines around her eyes spreading like cobwebs.

"Please, please take me to the bookstore."

"I'm going with Amani to the tea party. Ask your brother Aziz to take you."

3

"Yuba, you take me, may Allah save you."

Her father stood up and adjusted his black ogal over his white ghitra. "I have a meeting in half an hour. Ask Aziz."

"You're always like that!" Danah yelled, marching out of the living room. She flung her arms around her as if pushing away invisible objects obstructing her way. "You never have time for me. Never." She yelled the last word thrusting open the door of Aziz's room.

As usual, Aziz sat at his desk in front of the computer, as if nobody else in the house existed. "Danah, get out," he said, his eyes glued to the screen. His room was dark except for the desk light next to the computer.

"Mother said you should take me to the bookstore," Danah said, standing next to his desk. The computer displayed graphs and numbers, nothing fun or interesting.

"Not now, I have a class at the university this afternoon. I'll take you tomorrow." He dragged the mouse on the pad and clicked it twice.

"I need to go now!" Danah slammed the top of the monitor with the flat of her hand. The picture on the screen flickered.

Angrily, Aziz rose from his chair and pushed Danah roughly toward the door. "Don't ever do that. This is a computer not a toy."

Banging his door shut, Danah ran upstairs to her room. Nobody cared for her, nobody, she thought, pushing her door closed with both hands.

"And I don't like the curtains closed!" She pulled the curtain cord down, and drew the heavy wall to wall curtains open.

"What's going on here?" asked her mother at the door.

"Nothing," Danah mumbled.

Om Aziz had already changed into a fancy azure blue silk gown. The white beaded design around the collar made her dark face look brighter than usual. "Why don't you go with us to the party? There'll be girls your age there, I'm sure."

"Last time I believed you and what happened? I spent the whole evening listening to old women talk about how beautiful Amani will look in her wedding gown. "

Om Aziz sighed deeply. "So what are you going to do while we're gone?"

Danah shrugged. "I don't know. Maybe just play with the cat in the yard."

"Don't let her in the house though," her mother warned before she softly closed the door.

Danah went back to the window and looked outside. It was five in the afternoon and the sun was still high above, shining brightly behind the university buildings. The old henna tree in the backyard wilted under the heat and looked miserable.

Across the street, students who took summer classes, like Aziz, drove in and out of campus. Three more years, and she too would be a student there. Ooof, she could hardly wait. She would spend the whole day on campus away from her family. And if she missed them, she'd only have to look over at her house from the courtyard on campus, where the palm trees stood sentry. Then and there she wouldn't mind seeing the curtains of her bedroom closed all the time.

"Danah!"

Startled, Danah turned around. "You scared me," she said to Amani who stood gracefully at the door, all dressed up and looking as gorgeous as ever. An uneasy feeling stirred through her. "What do you want?"

"Are you sure you don't want to go with us?"

"Yes I'm sure. By the way, I don't like your hair like that."

Amani smiled touching her hair which she had neatly tied

up on the back. "You don't have to, Talal does." She pulled the door closed then opened it again. "By the way, didn't father tell you never to stand at the window?"

"None of your business," Danah yelled. She threw a pillow at the door but Amani was already gone.

———•◦•———

Around ten o'clock next morning, Danah ignored the knocking on her door.

"Don't you hear mother calling you?" Amani asked, pushing the door open.

"No," Danah said, waving her feet in the air as she lay on her stomach in bed. In front of her, on the pillow, was a book by one of her favorite American mystery writers.

"She's been calling you for the last ten minutes. Go see what she wants."

"I'm almost finished, wallah," Danah said without looking up. "Just one more page."

"No, you're not," Amani said, snatching the book from Danah's hand.

"Give me my book back!"

Amani grabbed a small mirror from Danah's dresser and held it in front of Danah's face. "Look at how ugly you look when you scream."

"I don't care, give me the book. I want to see who killed the clown."

Amani hid the book behind her back. "Go see what mother wants first."

Danah jumped on the bed. "Give me the book I said. Since when are you my supervisor? Just because you're getting married doesn't mean you…"

Amani pulled Danah by her pajamas, tickling her on the

6

stomach, her most ticklish spot. Danah giggled uncontrollably, and pushed and pulled Amani until they both landed on the floor, kicking and laughing.

"What a great sight," mother said, standing over them. "Amani, how would you like it if your future husband, Talal, would see you like that, ha?"

"I wish he does." Danah sat up on the floor, her curly hair all messed up over her eyes. "Maybe he'll change his mind about marrying her."

Amani slapped Danah on the arm. Then to her mother she said, "I just came to tell her you were calling." She scrambled up to her feet and left with Danah's book in her hand.

"Hey! Come back here and give me my book," Danah shouted.

"And you're not so young to act like that," Om Aziz said. "You're a grown up girl, and yet you're acting like a child."

"She took my book while I was reading," Danah protested.

"Aren't you tired of reading those books?" She picked up cushions and clothes from the floor and put them away.

"What else do you want me to do? It's my summer vacation, and everybody here is busy with Amani's wedding, Amani's wedding. As if I don't exist."

Om Aziz sat down on the dresser bench. "Which reminds me, your uncle called this morning from America."

"Uncle Faisal?" Danah smiled, showing a row of uneven teeth. "He's the only person in this whole world who cares about me."

"Stop being silly and listen. He suggested that you go visit him and his wife in August."

Danah rose up on her knees. "Visit them in America? Are you serious Yumma?"

"That's why I was calling you all morning."

"I'm sorry I didn't answer you, wallah."

"Now you're sorry, ha? So, what do you think? Do you want to go?"

Danah's thick eyebrows arched over her wide open eyes. "Do I want to go? Of course I want to go, but would father allow me to travel by myself?"

"I will convince him," Om Aziz said, smiling.

She looked pretty when she smiled, Danah thought returning her mother's smile. But suddenly her own smile vanished. "You only want to get rid of me, don't you?"

Om Aziz rose to her feet. "You know what? Forget the whole thing. You're not going anywhere." She marched out of the room.

Danah followed her down the stairway. "Wait! Wait, I'm sorry. Yumma, wallah, I'm sorry."

"You're so ungrateful," Om Aziz said shaking her forefinger in the air, "No matter what we do for you, you're ungrateful."

"I said I'm sorry!"

Om Aziz stopped at the bottom of the staircase and turned around. "What does that mean? Do you want to visit your uncle or did you suddenly become polite for a change?"

"I want to visit my uncle," Danah mumbled.

"Then go change your clothes and come downstairs to help me design invitation cards for Amani's…"

"Wedding, what else?"

"Move, and stop complaining."

Danah flew to her room, closed the door, and hopped on her bed. She jumped up and down on the mattress, waving her arms, really happy for the first time that summer.

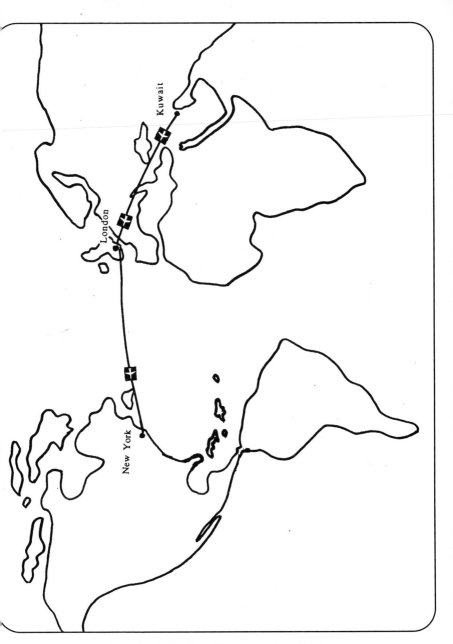

Danah's flight from Kuwait to New York.

CHAPTER TWO

July 29, 1990

*F*INALLY, THE DAY OF THE TRIP ARRIVED. Danah couldn't stop grinning all the way to the airport despite the miserable weather. A sandstorm swept over Kuwait City from the north, bringing hot, stinging wind. Her father, at the steering wheel, kept jamming the breaks thinking he was about to hit something he couldn't see from the drifting sand.

Amani sat next to Danah in the back seat of the black Mercedes. "Look at that silly smile." She pinched Danah on the arm. "You look so dumb smiling for no reason."

"For no reason?" Danah exclaimed. "This is going to be the best summer of my life and you say I'm smiling for no reason?"

"Let's hope you'll be grateful," Bu Aziz said as he gave a signal to turn into the airport entrance.

"And behave yourself, ha?" her mother said, turning around to look at Danah. "Don't embarrass us in front of your uncle's American wife, do you hear?"

Danah rolled her eyes. "Yes, yes, I hear. And you want me to keep my mouth shut so I won't bother them. You told me

11

that a million times. Zain, I will, wallah."

"Sure," Amani said. "Do you want to bet?"

"Yuba!" Danah called. "Listen to Amani she wants to bet with me."

Her father stopped the car in front of the passenger check-in gate. "Amani," he said as he turned off the engine. "You know betting is prohibited in Islam."

"I'm sorry Yuba, I was just teasing her." She opened the door and before she got out she looked at Danah. "And couldn't you find something better to wear than this striped t-shirt and those white jeans?"

"None of your business." Danah slid out of the car.

Inside the terminal, at the passport checkpoint, Danah hugged her father.

"Thank you Yuba."

He patted her on the shoulder. "Don't forget to recite the travel prayers before take off."

Danah turned toward her mother who was wiping her tears. "Ma'as salama, goodbye, Yumma." Danah kissed her on the cheeks.

"Ma'as salama habibti, take care of yourself, ha?"

"I'm going to miss you Danah." Amani hugged her tightly for a long moment. "Make sure you come back at the end of August, not later than that."

Danah laughed. "I know, I don't want to miss your wedding on the fifth of September."

———◆———

Inside the crowded plane, babies cried and veiled women tried to calm them down. Young men stood in the aisles, laughing and promising a game of cards in the back of the plane as soon as they took off.

12

At ten thirty sharp, the plane pulled away from the gate. Through the tiny window to her right, Danah watched the airport buildings move away from them. She bit her lower lip nervously. What if she would never see her family again? Something asked deep inside her. She shook her head, what a silly thought. Her father would never let such a thing happen. And thinking about her father, reminded her of the travel prayer he wrote for her on a piece of paper. She pulled it out of her pocket and read it silently.

Once the pilot had removed the seat belt sign a stewardess appeared. "Are you Danah Sa'eed?" she asked.

"Yes," Danah answered with a curious smile.

"Your father asked us to look out for you. Would you like something to drink?"

"No thank you," Danah said, relaxing in her seat.

Six hours later when the captain asked all passengers and crew members to prepare for landing at London's Heathrow airport, Danah began to worry again. Passengers continuing on to New York were requested to leave the plane for forty five minutes transit. What if she lost her way to the transit area?

A girl about twenty years old stopped at Danah's aisle. She wore a plain beige summer outfit, and brown framed eye glasses.

"Are you Danah Sa'eed?" she asked in a soft voice.

"Yes?"

"My name is Shatha. I am a friend of your sister Amani. She called me last night and asked me to give you company on the plane. I'm going to New York too."

"Alhamdu Lillah, thank God," Danah sighed with relief. "I was getting worried about losing my way through transit."

Shatha smiled. "Come, I'll show you where to wait."

Inside the transit lounge Danah and Shatha found a

quiet corner. "I don't remember Amani mentioning your name," Danah said.

Shatha nodded. "Amani and I took a required class together. My major is Literature. My cousin Rasha is a close friend of Amani's. That's how she knew I was taking the same flight as yours."

"Wait a minute," Danah exclaimed. "You must be the book-worm." After realizing what she said, Danah covered her mouth with both hands while studying Shatha's reaction to her indiscreet comment.

But Shatha only smiled. "Don't worry, I know they call me that behind my back because I like studying." She stood up. "They're calling us to go back to the plane. Let's go."

Inside the aircraft, Shatha asked the head stewardess if she and Danah could sit next to each other. When that was arranged the two girls settled in their seats giggling.

Danah took the window seat. "This is fun. So are you visiting a relative in America?"

"No, I am going to graduate school in Boston."

"Oof! Didn't you have enough of school?"

Shatha laughed. "I'm the book-worm, remember?"

After dinner was served and removed, the girls watched a comedy video then fell asleep for the rest of the trip.

The captain's deep voice asking everybody to prepare for landing pulled them out of their light sleep. Sitting up, they buckled their seat belts and looked out of the window. Streaks of evening light illuminated the sky and the tall buildings of New York City below.

"Allah!" Danah exclaimed, admiring the scene. "What's the time in New York?"

Shatha checked the time on her wrist watch. "Almost eight in the evening. Kuwait is seven hours ahead of New York. I

14

wonder if we can see the Statue of Liberty." After a brief search she sat back in her seat. "Ask your uncle to take you to Staten Island to see the statue. I was there with my family last year."

"All I want to see is Disney World." Danah clasped her hands together under her chin.

"But that's in Florida!"

"I know. My mother already asked my uncle to take me there, and he agreed."

Shatha waited until the plane touched down on the runway before she said, "I hope you'll have a good time there. "

"I'm sure I will," Danah said. She pulled her handbag from under the seat and got ready to leave the plane.

At customs, the tall gray eyed officer asked Danah if she was carrying any food.

"Just Arabian coffee and dessert."

"Let me see that please."

With Shatha's help, Danah lifted her suitcase to the table and opened the lock. Nervously, she watched the stranger's hands grope in her personal belongings: t-shirts, jeans, and night gowns. He finally pulled out the can of dessert.

"What's this?"

"Middle Eastern dessert," Danah said. She prayed he would not take away the only thing that her uncle had asked for.

After inspecting the contents carefully, the officer closed the can and put it back in the suitcase. The girls finally pulled their luggage away from customs.

Shatha stopped under a sign that said 'Connecting Flights'. "I have to take another flight to Boston now. I hope you'll find your uncle outside."

"I'm sure I will. And thank you so much Shatha, wallah."

Danah hugged her new friend. "I'll send you a card from Disney World, I promise."

Pushing her luggage cart, Danah found her way among the hundreds of arrivals toward the exit. The minute she passed the sliding doors she heard her uncle call her name. With a dancing heart, she spotted her Uncle Faisal's handsome face beaming at her in the middle of the crowd.

Danah let out a joyful scream before she hugged him. "I can't believe I'm actually here."

"Alhamdu Lillah, thank God for your safety," he said smiling. Then in English he said, "Let me introduce you to my wife, Julie."

With curious eyes Danah turned to look at the woman beside her Uncle. A tall blond lady stood smiling. Her perfect set of teeth were the whitest Danah had ever seen.

"Hi." Danah stretched a hand.

But Julie pulled Danah toward her and gave her a tight hug. "I'm so happy to meet you at last. Faisal talked about you more than anybody else in your family."

Uncle Faisal laughed. "I can't believe how much she's grown. Two years ago when I last saw her she was a tiny little thing. She's now almost as tall as you are."

"I wish," Danah said, standing on her toes next to Julie.

"You will be," Julie said. "You still have many years to grow, In Sha' Allah, God willing."

Danah felt her heart warming toward her uncle's wife. "In Sha' Allah," Danah repeated Julie's words.

"Let's go." Uncle Faisal grabbed the handle of Danah's cart and pushed it out of the terminal.

At eight in the evening, the air outside was warm and humid. At least it wasn't dusty, Danah thought, looking around. Green Kennedy airport terminal buses stopped to load and unload passengers. Yellow taxis waited in long lines to collect customers who themselves lined up for their turn to take one. Her uncle waited for some passing cars before he crossed the street to the parking lot. He led the way to his car among the hundreds of others parked in the parking area. Soon, they were on their way out of the busy airport.

From the back seat of the sporty Saab, Danah's eyes darted around trying to absorb everything all at once. Every once in a while she would glance at Julie, sitting in the front seat. She imagined herself describing her to Amani: "Julie's eyes are as blue as the sea, and her hair shines as bright as the sun on a clear day. She's tall and as white as Snow White. So now you're not the most beautiful girl in the family anymore."

"The first thing we'll do when we get back home," Uncle Faisal was saying in English, "is call your family. They must have called me a hundred times today, reminding me to pick you up from the airport."

Danah laughed. In Arabic she said, "I thought they'd forget me the minute I left."

CHAPTER THREE

New York City

UNCLE FAISAL AND JULIE LIVED in an apartment on the fifteenth floor. Upon arrival, Julie showed Danah a small room decorated with flowered wallpaper. "This is your room," she said.

Danah's inquisitive eyes studied the elegantly furnished room. An ornate Oriental carpet lay in the center of the polished oak floor. A poster bed with a cheerful yellow canopy faced a small desk. By the window was a wood rocking chair with painted flowers. A pleasant fresh fragrance hung in the air.

"It's beautiful, thank you," Danah said.

"Come on, I'll show you the rest of the apartment."

After the tour Danah stood in front of the huge windows in the living room and held her breath. "Julie, this is gorgeous."

"I know," Julie said proudly. "We love it. It wasn't easy getting an apartment with a view of Central Park, but it was worth waiting for." She then moved toward the kitchen. "Would you like something to eat?"

"No thank you, we ate on the plane."

"Danah!" Uncle Faisal called from his study. "Your mother's on the phone, she wants to talk to you."

"Yumma!" Danah yelled in the receiver. "You should come and see uncle's place. It is so beautiful."

"How are you?" her mother asked. "Are you tired? Was your flight all right?"

"I'm fine, let me talk to Amani."

"She's asleep, it's four-thirty in the morning here. Your father wants to talk to you."

Danah looked at the ship-clock behind her uncle's desk, nine-thirty in the evening, she should fix the time on her wrist watch. But her father's voice was getting louder. "Danah? Do you hear me? Give most of the cash to your uncle. It's not safe to carry it all in your purse."

"Zain, I told you I will do that."

"Take care of yourself, Zain?"

Danah rolled her eyes. "Talk to Uncle Faisal." She handed her uncle the receiver and walked out of the room.

"Would you like a piece of cake?" Julie asked from the kitchen.

"Yes, I'd like that." Danah leaned on the counter in the middle of the kitchen and watched Julie cut three pieces of chocolate cake. It reminded her of the different cakes and desserts her mother served every Thursday afternoon for tea with her women friends.

"You didn't stay long on the phone," Julie said, placing the pieces of cake in three separate plates.

"All they say is do this, do that, take care of yourself."

"That's because they love you." Julie handed Danah one of the plates and a fork.

"I don't know," Danah said with a mouthful of cake.

"Ummm..."

"Uncle Faisal," Danah said when her uncle joined them in the living room. "When are we going to Disney World?"

"Let's see," he said savoring a mouthful of cake. After swallowing it he added, "Guess what? I fooled you, we're not going anywhere. I just wanted you to come to visit."

Danah's fork fell on the wood floor, barely missing the Persian rug underneath the coffee table.

"Faisal?" Julie exclaimed with a smile.

Danah giggled and picked up the fork. "It's okay, wallah. I'm happy just to be here."

Uncle Faisal laughed his funny laugh which had always reminded Danah of a goat sound. Then he said, "You stinker, you always know what to say."

"Danah don't listen to him, he's just teasing you."

"He fooled me then," Danah said with a big smile, her uneven teeth covered with chocolate.

Uncle Faisal placed his empty plate on the coffee table and crossed his legs. "Today is Sunday the 29th of July. I took a week off work starting next weekend. We will leave Saturday morning, August 4th, and spend the whole week there in fantasy World."

"Yes!" Danah said. "Shukran Khali, thank you uncle. And thank you too Julie."

"Look at that happy face," Julie said laughing.

Danah covered her face with both hands. "I always wanted to visit Disney World. It is my dream."

"Well great," Julie said. "So your dream will finally come true. This week though, you and I will do a lot of bike riding in the park. Faisal told me you love bike riding."

Danah nodded, but there was a surprised look on her face. "You don't have a television?"

"It's inside that cabinet with the two doors," Julie said, pointing at a cherry wood entertainment unit by the window. "Do you want to watch something?"

"No," Danah said shaking her head.

Uncle Faisal smiled. "I know what Danah's thinking. See Julie, at home, in Kuwait, people switch the TV on, whether they are watching or not. And it stays on all day until it's time to go to sleep."

"Why?" asked Julie.

"It's a habit, maybe they like the sound of it in the background." Uncle Faisal looked at Danah who was suppressing a yawn.

Danah stood up. "I would like to go to sleep now."

Uncle Faisal looked at his watch. "That's not a bad idea, it's already eleven."

"Good night uncle. Good night Julie. I'm so happy I'm here. I could stay forever."

CHAPTER FOUR

August 1, 1990

AFTER BREAKFAST, JULIE LOOKED IN THE PHONE BOOK for bicycle shops. She called several places before they got in the car and visited a shop that sold used bikes. Danah tried several until they found one that fit her perfectly.

"For just one month this should do," Julie said as they pushed the bike to her Subaru station wagon.

"Thank you so much," Danah said cheerfully. "This is the first time anyone buys me a bike."

"I thought you had a bike!"

"No, I rode my brother's bike. My father refused to buy me one."

Julie and Danah carefully lifted the bike into the back of the car.

"I don't understand," Julie said as she backed out of the parking area. "I thought you had your own bicycle."

Danah shook her head. "See, when my brother Aziz started driving a car he never used his bike again. So I rode it around the yard. My parents would never let me ride it outside the house."

"Why not?"

"They say girls shouldn't ride bikes in the street. Maybe because boys will follow them or bother them."

"That's too bad. Well nobody should bother you here as long as you follow the rules for bike riding. Just like people follow rules when driving their cars."

"I can't wait," Danah said excitedly.

Danah didn't have to wait long. After Uncle Faisal left to work, Julie asked if she was ready for a bike ride.

"Yes!" Dana jumped off her chair at the breakfast table. She helped Julie put away the dishes, and quickly got ready to leave.

In the elevator to the garage, Julie handed Danah a shiny red bicycle helmet.

"Wear this for protection. It's mine, I think it'll fit you. I'll wear Faisal's." She helped Danah strap the helmet on, and then she wore hers.

The bikes were waiting where they had left them, locked to a bike rack in the garage. Julie unlocked the chain and they rolled the bikes out to the street.

Outside, the bright sun warmed the cool air that lingered from the early morning. Cars dashed by in the street between the building and Central Park. They waited for a horse-carriage carrying tourists to pass before they carefully crossed.

Inside the park, Julie stayed within the lines on the bike path, and signaled with her arms when she turned. Wanting to do the same, Danah wobbled and almost fell when she let go of the handle bar. She'd wait before she tried that again, she thought, smiling to herself. There were so many things to learn here.

After climbing a hill with great effort, Danah zoomed down the other side, following Julie closely. What a sensation of joy and freedom, Danah thought. This was an adventure she hadn't even dreamed of. But in just three days, she would be on her way to the adventure she had dreamed of for years.

"How are you doing?" Julie called.

"Okay."

"Are you tired?"

"A little." Danah tried to hide the panting from her voice.

"Let's stop here so you can rest." Julie slowed down before dismounting.

They sat on a bench facing a pond with ducks. Julie looked at Danah with a smile. "You're doing great. With time you'll get in shape to go on for hours."

Danah nodded and swallowed hard to wet her parched throat.

Julie laughed. "Tell you what, in an hour I'll take you to lunch at a beautiful place as a reward."

"Can we ride some more after that?"

Julie looked at her watch. "We can ride until four. I'd like to get home and prepare dinner before Faisal gets back from work."

"I'll help you cook." Danah smiled appreciatively at her uncle's wife. She wondered if all Americans were as nice as Julie.

During lunch Julie told her about the different ways to ride the bike so that she wouldn't get tired so soon. After lunch Danah practiced the tricks Julie told her, falling a couple of times. But that didn't discourage her, she got up immediately and tried over and over again.

Back in the apartment Danah had fun helping Julie make spaghetti with turkey sausages which she never had before. At home they only cooked spaghetti with ground beef. She then prepared the salad while Julie made dessert, Danah's favorite, rice crispie treats.

When they finished, Julie looked at the time. "Faisal is unusually late tonight. It's after eight."

The phone rang. "That must be him," Julie said running to answer it. "Hi Faisal, what's up?"

Danah watched Julie. She must truly love her uncle to be always thinking of him. A moment later however, Julie suddenly grew nervous while asking Faisal what time he was coming back home. She hung up, her face turned very pale.

"Is my uncle okay?" Danah asked.

Still standing by the phone, Julie repeatedly brushed her hair back with her fingers as she stared at the television cabinet. "Oh yes, he is. He said he'll be home in an hour." She inched toward the wood unit and opened the doors, picked up the remote control, pointed at the TV set but then changed her mind. She put the remote control down on the coffee table.

"Where does my uncle work?" Danah asked.

Absentmindedly, Julie walked to the kitchen and stood facing the refrigerator. "Oh, he works for Kuwait National Bank on Fifth avenue."

"Is it far?"

"No, not really." She then turned around to face Danah. "Why don't I serve you some food in case Faisal's very late."

Were those tears in her eyes? "Are you sure my uncle's okay?"

"Oh, he's okay." Julie tried to smile and brushed her eyes with the back of her hands.

"Then I'll wait to eat with you."

"I'm going to take a shower and change before he comes back? How about you?"

"I'll do the same thing," Danah said, walking to her room. But before she closed the door she heard the sound of the TV. When she glanced back toward the living room Julie was standing right in front of the TV set. Julie was suddenly acting strange, Danah thought. She said she was going to take a shower, instead she was watching TV? Everything had been fine before her uncle's call. What did he tell her?

Half an hour later Danah heard the door bell ring and Julie running to answer it. She almost ran to it too, but then she changed her mind. Laying down in bed, she opened *Les Miserables* which Julie bought for her the day before. Julie wanted her to read the book before they went to see the musical which was playing on Broadway. Danah flipped through the abridged version, then turned to the first page and started reading.

Another half an hour passed. She could hear the sound of the TV getting loud every once in a while, covering the voices of her uncle and Julie who quietly discussed something. During the first two evenings of her visit they only switched on the TV set after dinner, never before that. Perhaps she should join them.

In the living room, Julie and her uncle sat on the couch facing the TV. They were holding hands. When her uncle turned to look at her, Danah stopped smiling. His face was yellow, his eyes were red, he tried to smile but did a poor job of it.

"Shlonik Khali, how are you uncle?" Danah said in Kuwaiti Arabic. She sat down on a chair next to them, her eyes fixed on her uncle's sallow face.

"You should tell her Faisal," Julie said wiping away tears that suddenly flowed from her eyes.

Danah looked at the TV. A map filled the screen. The word 'Iraq' appeared on top. In the middle of the map many arrows pointed southward to another word: 'Kuwait'.

"What is it?" Danah asked Julie.

"Danah," her uncle finally said. "Iraq has just invaded Kuwait." He spoke in Arabic.

Blankly, Danah stared at her uncle's face, then at the screen. A serious looking news reporter appeared. He spoke rapidly repeating the word Kuwait and Kuwaitis many times. Danah didn't understand much besides that. But her uncle's face turned as white as a sheet of paper, tears gathered in his eyes.

"This cannot be true," Danah whispered. "Can it?"

CHAPTER FIVE

August 2, 1990

WHEN DANAH WOKE UP NEXT MORNING, she found her uncle sitting in the same chair he had occupied the night before. The living room was dark except for the light seeping through the edges of the closed curtains. He still wore the same clothes he was wearing the day before. Black marks lined his red eyes. The TV set displayed somber faces of reporters and government officials. In front of him, on the coffee table, sat the phone on top of an open phone book.

All the monstrous fears that Danah managed to push away during the night came back like iron chains wrapped around her. Dizzy and unable to breath, she leaned against the entrance unnoticed by her uncle. Perhaps she should go back to her room. But poor uncle, she wished she could make him feel better.

"Sabah alkhair Khali, good morning. Uncle," Danah finally said. She sat on the edge of a chair opposite him.

He switched on the lamp next to him and lowered the TV volume with the remote. "Did you get any sleep?"

"Yes, and you?"

"A little."

"Where is Julie?"

"She just went into the bedroom to get some rest."

Danah glanced at the screen before she asked, "So did the Iraqis leave?"

Her uncle shook his head. "No."

"Shall we call my parents to see how they're doing?"

Uncle Faisal stared at Danah for a long moment. "There are no lines to connect us with them any more."

Danah sucked in a brief gush of air. "Did you try?"

He nodded.

"Can I try?"

"I've tried all night, Danah. The Iraqis cut the international lines."

Danah picked up the phone. "Please, I want to try, tell me how."

"Dial 011- 965, and then the phone number."

Holding her breath, Danah dialed as her uncle told her. A recording immediately announced: "Due to the emergency situation in the country you're dialing, your call cannot be completed."

With the tears gathering in her eyes, Danah didn't see the table where she wanted to place the phone. It crashed to the floor. "Asfah, I'm sorry," she said picking it up. But her uncle didn't seem to notice. He had turned the volume up, his eyes glued again on the screen.

Danah quietly got up and went to her room. She sat on the bed and stared at her feet. She thought of the last time she talked to her parents, three days ago, when she arrived. She wasn't even nice to them. When her mother talked to her, Danah asked to speak to Amani, and when her father talked she gave the phone to her uncle. And worst of all, she complained to Julie about them.

Danah chewed on the inside of her lower lip. What was her family doing at that moment? What was Amani doing? Aziz? Her parents? Were they afraid? Were they safe?

"Danah?"

She looked up through her tears. Julie stood at the door, wrapped in her white robe, her hair disheveled. Danah tried to smile, but her chin only quivered.

"Are you okay sweetheart?" Julie touched Danah's hair.

Danah nodded still trying to smile.

"Would you join me for breakfast?"

Danah pulled herself up and followed Julie to the kitchen. "Faisal!" Julie called while taking milk and orange juice out of the refrigerator. "Please join us for breakfast, please?"

Uncle Faisal shuffled in. Danah took a deep breath before she asked him the question she dreaded to ask. "Would the Iraqis hurt the Kuwaitis?"

Uncle Faisal let out a deep sigh. "I hope not."

"I don't think they will," Julie said. "How can they? They're like brothers."

Uncle Faisal stood up. "I'm going to work."

After he left, Julie turned off the TV, opened the curtains and began dusting and polishing furniture. Danah stood in front of the window and gazed at the view fifteen floors below. Everything looked small and very far away. When Julie left the room, Danah picked up the phone and dialed her home number in Kuwait, but the same recording sounded again. She hung up and went to her bedroom.

Danah just finished reading the first chapter of *Les*

31

Miserables when Julie asked her if she wanted to go with her to the grocery store. "Do they sell greeting cards?" Danah asked.

"Yes, I think so. I'll show you where they keep them. Come on let's go."

At the supermarket, Danah chose a card that said, 'I Miss you'. She showed it to Julie saying, "Can we go to the post office? I'd like to mail this to my parents."

Julie kept quiet while putting the grocery bags in the trunk of her car. After she closed the trunk, she took Danah's hand in hers. "Perhaps you ought to wait a few days Danah, to see if mail will go through to your country."

"I don't see why mail should stop!"

"Who knows? But just like they stopped the phone lines, they might stop mail too."

"Can we try?"

Julie drove silently to the post office while Danah took out a pen from her purse and wrote:

'Dear Yumma and Yuba, I'm just writing to tell you that I miss you. I hope the Iraqis are not bothering you. How is Amani and Aziz? I love you, Danah.'

At the post office she stood in line with Julie until a clerk called on them. When Julie asked if they could send mail to Kuwait, the man shook his head and pointed at a flyer hung on the wall behind him. "We got this notice today to stop accepting mail going there."

"Why?" asked Danah.

"The Kuwaiti airport is closed."

Danah froze, the card clenched in her hand.

"Thank you," Julie said to the clerk. She put her arm around Danah's shoulders. "Let's go, Danah."

Danah stopped at the post office door. Did that mean she could never go back home anymore?

At the apartment, Julie suggested they go for a bike ride. Without saying a word Danah joined her in the elevator, wore the helmet, and pushed her bike out of the garage.

While riding in the park, Danah tried to understand what was going on. Iraq had invaded Kuwait. That was so hard to believe. Even if it was true, it could not last long because Iraqis would soon find out that they had made a mistake. They would realize that Kuwaitis were not their enemies. Besides, from her experience, she knew that adults tended to exaggerate things. Sometimes they would make a big deal out of nothing, just like when her parents found out that Iraqi troops had gathered at the borders months ago. They were so scared and worried, but then they seemed to forget all about it, nothing happened then, and things went back to normal.

Thinking that way made Danah feel better. She should not worry like adults do. She followed Julie on the bike, avoiding roller bladers and joggers speeding by.

Seeing her uncle's face later in the afternoon, her heart sank again. His face ghostly pale and eyes red, he looked totally shattered. He barely talked to her or Julie and a couple of times she thought he was talking to himself.

What amazed Danah the most, was that the news about Iraq and Kuwait was constantly discussed on American TV. But the more her uncle listened, the more depressed he became. As for her, she hardly understood anything more than Kuwait and Iraq, Americans spoke so fast.

Next morning, August third, Danah overheard Julie and Uncle Faisal argue in the living room.

"Saudi Arabia?" Julie asked. "Why?"

"Because my brother Usama is there. He called me last night and said many Kuwaitis who were out of Kuwait for summer vacation are gathering there now."

Then Danah heard him ask Julie if she would take her to Disney World without him. "My heart is not in it anymore."

"I understand, but I don't think we should go either. Not now."

"I know, but the poor girl…"

Danah rushed into the living room. "No Khali! We are not going without you. I'll wait until we can all go together."

"I agree with Danah," Julie said.

"So Khali." Danah sat down next to him. "Did the Iraqis leave Kuwait?"

Her uncle managed to smile, but Danah wished he would laugh his goat-like laugh that she loved so much. "Saddam is saying he will leave on Sunday. Let's hope he will."

CHAPTER SIX

August 4, 1990

Dear Amani,

It's Saturday night here, Sunday morning your time. Today, we were supposed to go to Disney World but we decided to wait until the Iraqis leave Kuwait. I hope by the time you receive this letter they will be gone.

Last night I dreamed of you wearing your wedding gown. You looked so beautiful in it, I can't wait to see you wearing it in real life. By the way, don't worry, I will not miss your wedding. I don't know when we will be going to Florida but I hope before August 29th, my return date.

Please say hello to Talal, your fiance. Also to Aziz, mother and father of course. See you in Kuwait, soon.

Your sister,
Danah

Dearest Amani,

I cannot believe what is happening. Yesterday, I watched the news with my uncle and Julie and asked them to translate for me. I was expecting the Iraqis to leave our country like they said they would . But they didn't. Uncle Faisal is now even more upset than he was before. He says the Iraqis are there to stay. Amani do you believe that? I don't , I can't. And what about me? How can I see you again? And what about your wedding?

I think of you and Aziz and my parents all the time. I wish I can be with you, even with the Iraqis there, I don't care. But I don't know how, Julie says they are not letting anyone enter Kuwait. The airport and the borders are closed.

Amani, last night I read an article in the New York Times , I couldn't believe what they said.

They said that the Iraqi soldiers are killing Kuwaitis. I got so scared, I didn't sleep all night. Now I'm worried about all of you, how can I know that you are safe? I also wonder if I'm ever going to see you again, if I'm ever going to see mother and...

"Danah!" Julie rushed in the room. "What is it?"

Danah covered her face with both hands while gasping for breath. The pen still clutched between her fingers.

Julie sat next to her on the bed, and tried to calm her with soothing words but that only made Danah cry more. When Julie hugged her, Danah imagined she was hugging her mother like she had at Kuwait airport just a week ago. "Yumma, ana asfah yumma, I'm sorry."

Julie's arms tightened around her. "Calm down sweetheart. Calm down."

Danah gasped for air. "What …I thought."

"Shsh… you are a strong girl Danah and you should stay that way especially during this difficult time."

Danah wailed. "But my father … Aziz…"

"Just pray that they will be safe."

Danah closed her eyes tightly and recited verses from the Koran. She prayed to God to save her family and all Kuwaitis from the Iraqis.

Julie handed Danah a Kleenex. "Now why don't you come out of your room and give me some company. I missed you all morning."

Danah wiped her tears. "I'll wash my face and join you."

"Let's go for a walk," Julie suggested when Danah walked into the living room.

In the park, tourists still walked around with their cameras, laughing and taking pictures of each other. Joggers and bikers zoomed around just like they had before the invasion of Kuwait, as if nothing had happened. Danah wished she had Aladdin's magic carpet, she would fly back home. With his magic lamp she would push the Iraqis out of her country.

"So how come your parents called you Danah?" Julie was asking her. "To me it sounds like a western name."

"It's an old Kuwaiti name. It means the big pearl."

A tear dropped out of Danah's eye as she remembered her father saying, "You are the pearl of all pearls."

"Is there a name for a small pearl?"

"Yes, Gumashah."

"Oh that's different, but I understand it since pearl diving was what Kuwaitis did before oil was found."

"My great grandfather was a pearl diver. My father still

remembers stories he used to tell him."

"That's so neat," Julie said. "Do you remember any of them?"

Danah thought for a moment. "I remember how much my grandfather loved those days. He used to say Kuwait was so quiet and peaceful then. Kuwaitis were so poor, yet so generous. I remember him shaking his head and saying, 'I wish oil was never found.'"

Danah shook her head and tried to mimic her grandfather's voice saying those words she remembered so well. Then she frowned and said,"I didn't understand what he meant then, but now I think I do."

CHAPTER SEVEN

August 9, 1990

"**I**'M THINKING OF WRITING AN ARTICLE about the false Iraqi claims on Kuwait," Julie said as she vigorously folded a newspaper she was reading at the New York Public library.

"What?" Danah pulled herself back from Khaledeya, her residential district in Kuwait. She had been thinking of the public library there. Even though she had visited the tiny library only once for school research it popped in her mind the minute she and Julie walked into the New York Library an hour earlier. There was no comparison in terms of the building or number of books. Yet, just being there reminded her of the two-room library back home, with its distinctive aroma of cardamom and saffron tea the librarian used to drink. Would he still open the library now that the Iraqis had taken over?

"Can we write a protest letter to the Iraqi Embassy?" Danah asked.

"We can do that too," Julie said. "Why don't you write down what you have in mind and I'll edit it for you."

Danah opened her notebook and began writing a letter to

the Iraqi Ambassador in Arabic. She would translate it to English later.

Julie brought a stack of books to the large table and began researching. She read and took many notes. Three hours later she closed the books. "It's time to go. I've got some errands to run, would you like to go with me?"

"Can you take me to the apartment?" Danah closed her notebook and put away her pen. "I'll read in *Les Miserables* until you come back."

"Sure, it's on my way. Let's go."

At the apartment, Danah stood in front of the living room windows looking at the park. She wondered who was more miserable now, Cossette in *Les Miserables* or herself? She wondered what her family was doing at that moment. It must be night there. Were they afraid? Did they really have food like Uncle Faisal told her? She knew there were many things happening over there that Julie and her Uncle kept from her. She tried to listen and understand the news reports on CNN, but by the time her mind translated the first part of the report, the rest was already over.

Danah turned toward her room when she spotted the phone. She picked it up and dialed her home phone number. Still the same recording: "Due to the emergency situation in the country..." She knew it by heart, she didn't need to listen to the end of it. Placing the phone back down on the coffee table, Danah noticed her notebook next to it. On the cover was the phone number and address of the Iraqi Embassy that Julie had copied from a big phone book in the library. They planned to mail the protest next day after Julie typed it.

Without thinking Danah dialed the number of the embassy. A voice of a man came through immediately. "Halloo?"

"Is this the Iraqi embassy?" Danah asked in Arabic.

Also in Arabic but with a strong Iraqi accent the man said, "Yes, how can I help you?"

Suddenly anger and resentment surged in Danah's head. "How can you help me? Get out of Kuwait, that's how you can help me. Get out, what you've done is wrong."

The man remained quiet for a moment before he said, "If you calm down we can discuss what's bothering you. First of all who are you?"

"I am a Kuwaiti."

"Well, first of all, you are not a Kuwaiti anymore. You are now an Iraqi, and you should be proud of it."

"God forbid," Danah shrieked. "I am a Kuwaiti and will always be a Kuwaiti as long as I live. You should be ashamed of yourselves and stop being so arrogant. What you've done is wrong."

"Why are you saying that? Where do you get your information? From the news? What they're saying is not true."

"I'm getting my information from the fact that I cannot go back to see my family or talk to them…" Danah choked on her tears.

"That's no problem," the man said calmly. "I can arrange it so that you can go back to see your family as soon as you wish."

"You are a liar!" Danah yelled before slamming the phone down.

As if the Iraqi man might materialize out of the phone to follow her, Danah ran to her room and locked the door firmly. She sank down on the chair by the window and chewed hard on the inside of her lip. But what if the man was serious and could actually take her to her family? It might be her only chance to see them. She should have asked him how he would

41

take her there instead of calling him a liar. Perhaps she should call back?

While Danah debated whether or not she should call the man back the phone rang. She jumped to her feet. That must be her uncle or Julie checking on her so now she could ask them their opinion. She dashed to the phone in the living room. But the thought that it might be the Iraqi man calling her back made her stop as if the receiver was going to burn her hand. She stared at the phone as it rang persistently. Her family at home was facing the Iraqis in person on a daily basis, and here she was worried to deal with one over the phone? She picked it up.

"Danah?" a young female voice said.

With a sigh of relief Danah answered, "yes!"

"I am Shatha, remember me?"

"Of course I remember you," Danah exclaimed, the tension on her shoulders gradually lifting. "How are you?"

"I'm fine. I called to tell you that tomorrow I'm leaving to Saudi Arabia to stay with my brother and his family. Do you have somebody there that I can deliver a message to?"

Danah's mind started sorting out many things all at the same time. "Wait, wait. First why are you going there? You think you can enter Kuwait?"

"I don't think so, the Iraqis are not allowing anyone to enter Kuwait. See, I'm all by myself here. I think I'll feel better with my brother and his family."

"Do you have a ticket to go to Saudi Arabia?"

"My ticket is for going back to Kuwait, but Kuwaiti and Saudi airlines are accepting those tickets to take Kuwaitis back to Saudi Arabia or the Emirates."

"You mean I can use my ticket to do the same thing?"

"Yes, I'm sure. Is your family there now?"

"No," Danah said recalling a discussion between her uncle and Julie a few nights before. "I think my Uncle Faisal said that his brother, Uncle Usama is in Saudi Arabia."

"Are you thinking of going there?"

"No. Yes. I mean, I am now. Which flight are you taking tomorrow?"

Danah wrote down the information Shatha gave her and hung up. She paced around the living room several times before she stood in front of the windows overlooking Central Park. People still walked their dogs, joggers ran the winding path, horse-carriages slowly moved along the street carrying happy tourists in the back. But it felt so wrong to be watching such a beautiful scene when her family was in danger. To be in Saudi Arabia closer to her family felt more like the right thing to do.

At that moment Julie walked through the entryway.

"Hi Danah!" she sang out cheerfully before she stopped. "Are you okay?" she asked with a worried look on her face.

Danah smiled. "I just got a phone call from Shatha, the girl I met on the plane."

Julie sat down on the couch. "You look like you've just seen a ghost. Come and sit down next to me." She patted the seat next to her on the couch. "Tell me about her call. I hope she didn't give you any bad news."

Danah chuckled as she sat next to Julie. "She told me she's leaving to Saudi Arabia tomorrow."

"Sure, I understand if she's all alone here."

Danah nodded, kept quiet for a minute then said, "I'd like to go with her."

"To Saudi Arabia?"

"Yes."

"Why?" Julie asked.

"I'm hoping my family will leave Kuwait like many others. I'd like to be there to meet them when they do."

Julie didn't seem convinced but after a long moment of silence she said. "I know exactly how you feel, Danah."

Uncle Faisal suddenly opened the main door. "Salam Alaikum," he said at entering the living room.

"Alaikum asalam," Julie and Danah answered together.

"What's going on?" he asked looking at them closely.

"Sit down honey," Julie said. "Danah wants to tell you something."

"No," Uncle Faisal said firmly when Danah told him her plan. "I would not hear of it."

"But Uncle Usama is my uncle too," Danah said.

Uncle Faisal kept quiet. It took Julie and Danah a long time to finally convince him to let Danah go to Saudi Arabia. He said he would let her go on the condition, that Danah would stay with his brother, Uncle Usama, not with Shatha's family.

"Who knows?" he said looking at Julie. "Perhaps I'll be there soon too."

Danah hugged her uncle.

"Give me the information on Shatha's flight," he said, patting her shoulder. "I'll make sure you get a seat next to her."

CHAPTER EIGHT

August 10, 1990

DANAH AND JULIE CRIED AT THE AIRPORT as they said good-bye. Uncle Faisal stared at them with glossy eyes. With his hands in his pockets, he watched as if he was just another passenger.

"Thank you very much for everything, Julie," Danah said. "I'm sorry I can't go with you to see *Les Miserables.*"

"Me too, but it's okay. I hope you'll get to see your family instead."

Danah then hugged her uncle. "Thank you Khali."

"Take care of yourself, zain?" he said.

Danah shuffled toward the gate which was flashing a 'Boarding' sign. But before she stepped into the tunnel, Julie called her to wait.

"I forgot to give you this." Julie handed Danah a blue cap that said 'Disney World' on it. "I want you to have it as a souvenir, even though you didn't get to go."

Danah smiled. She traced the colorful stitched letters on the cap with her fingers. "Thank you."

Julie touched Danah's cheek lightly. "Maybe next summer everything will be back to normal. We'll take you then?"

"In Sha' Allah. I'll write to you." She waved goodbye one last time before she walked through the tunnel.

Inside the Kuwaiti aircraft a stewardess showed Danah to her seat next to Shatha's. The girls had already met at check in when Uncle Faisal made sure they were assigned seats together. Danah wore the cap Julie gave her and slouched down into her seat.

Shatha gazed at Danah. Her puffed eyes behind her thick glasses looked smaller than Danah remembered. "Did you bring an abaya with you to wear over your clothes?"

Danah checked her slacks and blouse as if she saw them for the first time. "Why?"

"Because in Saudi Arabia you cannot walk outside dressed like that."

"So what can I do?" Danah asked apprehensively.

Shatha thought for a moment. "I'll ask my brother's wife if she has an extra one to give you." She then nodded at the cap. "Did you go there?"

"No. It's a gift from Julie."

"She seems to be a very nice lady," Shatha said.

"She's great," Danah said. "Are all Americans like her?"

"Most of those I met at the university are very nice. Look how they're sympathizing with us." Shatha pointed at pictures of American soldiers in the Arabic newspaper she held.

Danah grabbed the paper like a thirsty person would grab a glass of water. "I can finally understand what's going on. Is this a Saudi paper?"

"Yes. You can have it. I have another one."

Danah's eyes scanned the headlines printed in large Arabic letters: Fifty thousand American soldiers deployed to Saudi Arabia. Fear of hunger and starvation in Kuwait. Thousands of

Kuwaitis flee to Saudi Arabia. Reports of killings and destruction in Kuwait.

The words on the paper swam across the page as tears gathered in Dana's eyes. She quickly wiped them away and began reading the articles. A heavy burden gathered on her shoulders, making them droop over the paper.

When the captain asked passengers and crew to get ready for take off, Danah sat up, removed the Disney cap off her head and placed it in her handbag. She buckled her seat belt and looked around at the passengers, mostly young Kuwaiti men. How different the scene looked from the last time she had been on the plane. The passengers' sad faces showed shock and fatigue from sleepless nights of worry over their unknown future. How helpless they must feel. Yet, worst of all, was the fear for the lives of dear ones, who were now prisoners in their own land.

"What are we going to do?" Danah asked Shatha who stared out the window.

"I don't know. I'm hoping they will let me do some work to help the soldiers."

"Like what?"

"Cooking or cleaning, or anything. I just want to help."

Danah pondered over Shatha's words. She too would like to help. But how?

"Have you heard from your family since the invasion?" Shatha asked her.

"No, not a word."

"Neither have I. My brother said that most Kuwaitis in Saudi Arabia are camping at the border with Kuwait. They're hoping their relatives would leave. Those who leave Kuwait sometimes bring letters and news from relatives who stayed behind."

"Is your brother going there?"

"Yes. I'm hoping he'll take me with him."

Danah wondered if her Uncle Usama would join the camp

at the borders too. She imagined waiting there, watching the people drive through the borders and spotting her family. Her heart skipped a beat as she thought of how she would run to them. Amani in the back seat of their car would recognize her and tell her father to stop. Her mother would jump out of the car to meet her. Danah closed her eyes tightly, hoping to keep that image in her mind, praying that it would come true.

During the rest of the trip Danah and Shatha read quietly and dozed off dreaming similar dreams. When they arrived at Riyadh International Airport in Saudi Arabia, hopes of their dreams coming true were kindled by what they saw. The airport bustled with confident American and Saudi soldiers. Many Kuwaiti passengers were met by proud young men wearing military uniforms.

Danah and Shatha had to wait in a long line for quite a while. Security officials checked baggage with large German shepherd dogs that sniffed each suitcase and handbag for bombs. Finally, they were able to walk out of customs to hundreds of relatives who waved and shouted for their loved ones.

"Danah! Danah! Over here!"

Far in the back of the mass of people was her Uncle Usama whom she vaguely remembered from the last time they had met years ago. How unlike Uncle Faisal he looked. He seemed much older and had many wrinkles on his forehead. Perhaps the recent events had aged him. Like most men around them, he wore a white dishdasha and a white ghitra on his head, held in place with a black ogal.

Danah hurriedly said goodbye to Shatha and maneuvered through the crowd toward her uncle. He briefly shook her hand, grabbed her luggage and led the way to the exit doors. Before stepping out, Uncle Usama handed Danah a black abaya.

"Wear this," he said flatly. "You cannot walk outside without it."

Danah struggled with the silky material as she searched for the arm holes on the sides. That was the first time she ever wore one. Neither her mother nor Amani wore the abaya or the veil, but some of her women relatives and friends did.

Her uncle led the way to a parking lot decorated with palm and other familiar looking trees. Just like home, Danah thought with a smile. But her smile disappeared when they drove alongside military vehicles out of the airport. Hundreds if not thousands of jeeps and trucks carrying weapons moved down the highway.

"Don't worry," her uncle said noticing her anxiety. "Saddam wouldn't dare to bomb us with the Americans here."

But that thought hadn't even occurred to her. What did all the military machinery mean? Was there going to be a war? What would happen to her family then? Would she ever get to see them? Or was that going to be another unfulfilled dream this summer, like visiting Disney World?

When they passed the Riyadh City exit, her uncle announced, "We're staying at one of the hotels where the Saudi Government is putting up the Kuwaiti refugees."

Danah winced at the word 'refugees'. It never occurred to her before that a person's status could change to a refugee overnight. She herself was a refugee now, Danah thought, finding the idea difficult to take. She gathered the black abaya tightly around her.

At the hotel Danah found out that Shatha and her family were staying in the same hotel. Not only that but Uncle Usama and Shatha's brother had already met and planned to leave to the Kuwaiti borders and camp there for a few nights.

"Can I go with you, please, uncle Usama?" Danah begged him that night.

"Is Shatha going?" he asked.

"Yes, she told me they're all going, even the children."

"You think you can handle camping there in the desert?" he asked, looking at her with weary eyes.

"Yes, wallah."

"So make sure you wake up very early. We are leaving at dawn."

"Is your wife going too?"

"No. My wife's parents left Kuwait a few days ago. She's staying with them in her relative's house in Riyadh."

"Do you think my family will leave too?" Danah asked anxiously, hoping somehow he knew something.

"Only God knows."

The next morning Danah and Shatha sat together in the back seat of her uncle's Chevrolet Impala. They gazed listlessly at the slick long desert road that would take them closer to home. Shatha's brother and his family drove behind maintaining the same speed. Hours later, both cars slowed down as a huge camp appeared in the distance. Enormous gray canvas tents spread over acres of desolate desert. Green army trucks lined the road ahead of them.

At the camp, hundreds of cars with Kuwaiti license plates were parked everywhere. Crowds of women wearing black abayas wandered around in a confused manner. Groups of men would suddenly congregate in one area and just as suddenly disperse to another. Saudi soldiers surrounded the camp trying to maintain order. At a speed of ten miles per hour Uncle Usama and Shatha's brother advanced on the road, still going north.

Finally, a Saudi guard stood in the middle of the road waving at cars to turn around. "Can we park somewhere here?" Uncle Usama asked the soldier.

"Back at the camp." The soldier pointed with his finger. "You cannot park here anymore."

Driving back about three miles, and finding a parking spot took almost an hour. Around noon, they finally stepped out of the car to stretch. Hot desert air lashed at their wet faces. The two men, Uncle Usama and Shatha's brother Yusef, asked the women to wait by the car until they checked with the authorities for permission to stay.

Danah wondered how she would ever spot her family in such confusion. She walked with Shatha toward Yusef's car, struggling to keep the abaya over her head. She admired the way Shatha kept hers steady over her head while she gracefully moved under the black shroud.

Shatha's two little nieces came running toward them. "Mother says come and eat with us," one of the girls said.

The men returned with permission from the Saudi authorities to stay at the camp. There was no separate housing for each family. Women stayed together in one area, the men in another. Yusef, Shatha's brother, asked his wife if she preferred to go back to Riyadh and wait in the comfortable hotel since she was eight months pregnant. She wept. No, she'd wait for her family no matter what the conditions were like.

"But there is no guarantee that your parents will leave," he said.

"At least somebody might bring us some news about them." She sobbed.

"Zain. Zain," Yusef said resignedly. "Let's stay two nights and see what happens."

The men locked up the cars and carried a few small handbags. They all shuffled slowly through the sand. Danah followed Shatha who followed her sister-in-law to one of the huge tents pitched in the women's area where they would spend the night, so close to her family, and yet so far away.

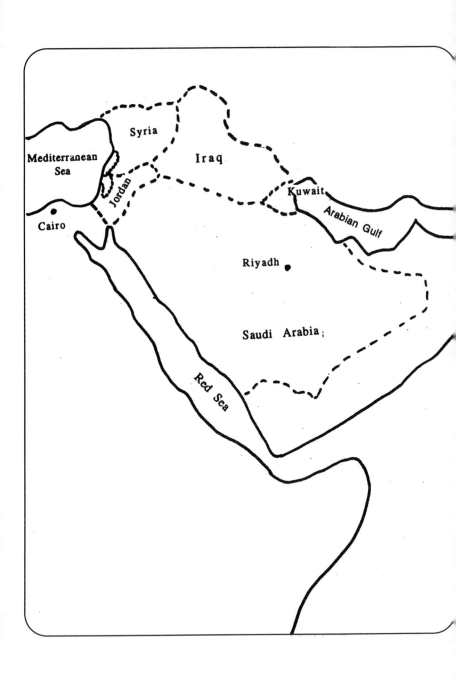

CHAPTER NINE

August 12, 1990

SLEEP IN THE CAMP WAS IMPOSSIBLE. Wrapped in the thin abaya, Danah lay awake on the dirt floor next to Shatha in the middle of the dimly lit tent. A layer of dust mixed with sweat covered her face, like the worry that weighed upon her heart. She listened to women and children weep, while others moaned like wounded prisoners.

At different intervals of the night more refugees arrived. Some women who could not sleep treaded toward them. They asked anxiously about the latest news from inside Kuwait. Danah couldn't help but join them.

"Iraqi soldiers are capturing all Westerners they find inside Kuwait and take them to Baghdad," one young lady said. Her abaya fell to her shoulders uncovering her tousled hair. Fatigue and exhaustion lined every part of her thin face.

A woman brought her a glass of water. "Why are they doing that?"

The young lady swallowed a sip of water. "Because of the embargo. They're also afraid that the U.S. will attack. There are rumors that the Iraqis are taking the hostages to their military centers in Baghdad to use them as human shields."

Everybody kept quiet thinking of what they just heard. Then one woman asked, "How are the Kuwaitis doing?"

The young lady gulped the remainder of the water. "Some are scared and are hiding inside their homes, some are getting ready to leave. Yesterday, I joined a group of women in a peaceful demonstration holding up pictures of the Emir. The Iraqi soldiers opened fire on us, I was lucky I didn't get hurt but many women got injured and one died. That's when I agreed with my husband it was time to leave."

Shock and horror at that piece of news kept the women from asking any more questions. What if their sisters or relatives were among those women in the demonstration? What if it was their mother or sister who got killed?

"What is the name of the woman who died?" Danah heard herself ask.

"I don't know." The woman shook her head.

Danah went back to her spot and lay down, covering herself with the black abaya. What if Amani had joined the women in the demonstration? What if she was …? Danah pulled the abaya up over her head, as if to keep those awful thoughts away from her mind. She prayed earnestly to God to keep her family from harm. She recited prayers her mother had taught her when she was little, whenever she got scared at night.

A few hours later, when light began seeping into the tent from outside, Danah sat up. She found Shatha sitting next to her, quietly crying. "What is it?" Danah touched her friend's shoulder.

"Nothing. I had a nightmare." Shatha wiped her tears with a Kleenex. She put her glasses back on her face and pulled her hair back in a pony tail. "I need to get some fresh air," she said standing up.

Wrapped in their abayas, the girls carefully made their way out among women who were stretched out on the floor in hope of catching some sleep. Outside, the golden light of the early sun illuminated the eastern horizon. Danah filled her lungs with fresh clean morning air. She glanced at the time on her wrist watch, almost six o'clock.

Uncle Usama and Yusef were already awake. They sat on the car hood, their white ghitras piled on top of their heads, their dishdasha sleeves rolled up to their elbows. They gazed north, toward home.

Salwa, Yusef's wife, sat inside the back seat of the car with her two daughters. Her eyes and nose were red and swollen. "Sabah al Khair, good morning." She tried to smile as she greeted Danah and Shatha.

They stood close to the front of the car and listened to the two men discussing the rounding up of foreigners in Kuwait by the Iraqis. Danah wondered if she should tell them about the women's demonstration. But she decided against it, why make them worry?

"And how can they open fire on a group of unarmed women?" Shatha's brother Yusef said.

So they already heard, Danah thought. She sadly looked at Shatha whose eyes instantly filled with tears again. Danah couldn't stop her own tears from flowing down.

Uncle Usama jumped off the car hood. "I'm going back to the nearest town to buy food and water. Danah do you need anything?"

She shook her head.

"I'll go with you." Yusef followed Uncle Usama to his car.

A sudden commotion by a group of women at the tent

55

drew Danah's attention. Two women ran out of the tent toward the north side of the parking lot. There, a woman wearing a face cover as well as the abaya over her head, carried two children and urged three more tramping behind her to hurry up. The other women swooped down on them and helped the mother carry the youngest children back to the tent.

Danah and Shatha exchanged a quick glance before they rushed to the tent. Inside, the new arrivals sat in the middle of a huge group of eager women. Danah drew as close as she could and peered at the mother who had pulled the burga' off her face and abaya off her head. She wore a colorful long gown, her hands painted with henna, two dozen golden bracelets clattered on her wrists.

Everyone around the woman repeated the same expression, "Alhamdu Lillah ala salama. Thank God for your safety."

Pulling the youngest of her children to her lap, the mother thanked the women profusely. She rocked the child urging him to go to sleep.

"Who is she?" Shatha asked the woman next to her.

"Om Thamer," the woman whispered. "She was with her husband here in Saudi Arabia when the invasion happened. Her children were in Kuwait alone."

"Alone?" Danah asked.

"She has a fifteen year old son who takes care of his sisters and brothers when his parents come here. See," the woman lowered her voice, "they are Kuwaiti bedouins. They have cattle that graze not far from the borders."

"So how did she get her children out?" Shatha asked.

The woman smiled. "That's what's amazing. She was going crazy the first few days of the invasion without her children. Finally, Bu Thamer, her husband, decided to go back inside Kuwait through the desert avoiding the official border."

"And he made it back with the children?" Danah whispered.

"Yes, isn't it wonderful?"

"Yes, it is," said Danah, wondering if anybody else would try to do the same thing again.

CHAPTER TEN

August 21, 1990

*D*URING THE NEXT FEW DAYS Danah made friends with Om Thamer's eldest daughter. Zainah was eleven years old and had to take care of her three year old sister Farah. Her mother took care of the two youngest boys.

Danah tried to help Zainah take care of her sister. When Farah slept, Danah asked Zainah questions that had troubled her since the invasion.

"Was it scary to hear the Iraqis storm in?"

"Of course it was scary," Zainah said with a distinctive bedouin accent which Danah thought was charming. "But what is more scary is the feeling, how can the Iraqis our brothers and neighbors do such a thing? That's more than scary."

"Did you see them?"

"Of course we saw them. The first few days we only heard them because we live in Hadiya, far from the city. We heard their planes and helicopters. We could hear them pound and blow up places in the city."

"Then what happened?" Danah asked, her heart throbbing.

"Then after a few days we started seeing them in their tanks and trucks moving south. They left some of their soldiers in Hadiya but the rest kept moving south."

Danah hesitated before she asked, "Did they bother you?"

"Of course they bothered us. Just seeing them bothered us. But they came over to our house once and asked Thamer my brother for food and water."

"I'm glad you're safe Zainah," Danah said, fear forming inside her, like a real object.

The next few days brought bad news to everyone waiting at the camp. First, the Iraqi soldiers, realizing that Kuwaitis were helping foreigners leave Kuwait through the desert to Saudi Arabia, began shooting haphazardly at Kuwaiti vehicles moving south away from checkpoints. The other piece of news which outraged and shocked everybody was that while people waited in their cars at the borders to be admitted to Saudi Arabia, an Iraqi military truck drove up, pulled two young Kuwaiti men out of their car, shot and killed them in front of their mothers and relatives.

Danah couldn't stop crying all day over that piece of news.

In the evening, Uncle Usama tried to calm her down when Shatha's efforts failed. He sat next to her on the sand outside the tent and tried to make her talk to him. But all she said was, "Why? Why?"

"Because the Iraqis suspected them to be part of the resistance movement," he said.

Danah sobbed even more as she imagined her brother Aziz getting out of the car and confronting the soldiers with their guns ready to shoot. She wailed, "But they didn't do anything wrong. They were just defending our country."

"That's true. But the Iraqis didn't want them to do that."

"So they kill innocent people? Innocent people?" Danah

covered her eyes as she imagined the soldiers firing at Aziz. Her heart ached as she saw him explode splattering blood all over the white desert sand.

Uncle Usama stood up and wiped his face with his ghitra. "Listen Danah, tomorrow morning we're leaving back to Riyadh."

"No, please," Danah pleaded, finally lifting her head from her knees.

"I don't think your family or mine will leave Kuwait after hearing what's happening at the borders. Besides, I have left my wife and children long enough back in Riyadh."

"Then you can leave, I'll stay with Shatha's family."

"No! I'm sorry Danah, but you have to leave with me." He walked away before she could answer him.

Danah put her head back down on her knees. Being at the borders with Kuwait made her feel close to her family. They breathed the same air, heard the same news. That was the closest she had gotten to her family since she had left them. To take her away now would be like pulling her arm out of her body. It would hurt too much. But no one could understand, no one. She sobbed quietly.

A hand suddenly touched her hair and forehead. Danah slowly lifted her head up. It was Farah, Zainah's three year old sister. "Ta'ali, come," she said, taking Danah's hand.

Zainah sat down on the sand next to Danah. "Farah was looking for you all day."

Danah hugged the little girl, hiding her tearful face in the tiny chest.

"Poor girl," Zainah said. "Everywhere she goes people are crying."

Danah pulled out a Kleenex from her pocket, wiped her

eyes and blew her nose. "How can you blame us?" She placed Farah in her lap.

"Of course I don't. Especially my poor mother," Zainah choked back her tears. "My father told her this morning he wants to go back into Kuwait. She's begging him not to. But my father won't listen."

Danah couldn't hide her curiosity. "Why does he want to go?"

"He gave his word to our neighbors that he'd go back and help them get out."

"Is your brother Thamer going too?"

"He wants to, but my mother won't let him. My father told him one man should stay behind with the family in case something happens to him." Zainah's tears streamed down her cheeks.

Danah took Zainah's hand. "Farah must think you are the bravest one of us for not crying. You shouldn't let her down."

Zainah brushed her tears with the back of her hands. "Of course I'm not the bravest."

"To me you are Zainah," Danah said. She played with a strand of Farah's hair. "When is your father leaving?"

"Tonight, at two in the morning."

Shatha's voice sounded from the tent entrance. "Danah! Don't you want to eat?" She walked toward them. "Danah you haven't eaten all day. Yusef just brought us warm sandwiches for dinner. You too Zainah, come join us."

Inside the tent women gathered in groups around their scanty dinners. Danah took a sandwich that Salwa handed her and chewed on it absentmindedly. Someone was actually going inside Kuwait. She glanced toward Zainah's group. All the women were eating except Om Thamer, Zainah's mother. Rocking her youngest son in her lap, she held a handkerchief over her eyes with her other hand. She refused to listen to her daughter's and friends' pleas to have a bite.

Poor lady, Danah thought. After gathering her family safely together she would be worried again. But who wasn't worried? Danah looked around at the faces of girls and women. Not one single smile. Not even on the children's faces.

One of Shatha's nieces skipped over to Danah and handed her an orange. "Shukran habibti." Danah took the orange and gave the girl a kiss.

"I need to go to the car to get something from my hand bag," she announced.

"I'll go with you," Shatha said. "Do you have the car keys?"

"My uncle leaves the car unlocked. No one around here would think of stealing anything from anybody."

"That's true," Shatha said.

Faint streaks of pink and purple remained on the western horizon where the sun sank earlier. Serious voices of men sounded from the other side of the camp. Some sat on the hoods of their cars, gazing pensively north, as if they expected somebody to suddenly appear.

At her uncle's car, Danah opened the back door and reached for her handbag. She zipped open the bag and put the orange in it. What else was in there? She searched through the items in the bag. On top was the cap Julie gave her. Underneath it was *Les Miserable* and her notebook in which she wrote letters to Amani. At the bottom was a copy of the *New York Times* in which Julie's article about the invasion was published. Tucked in a zipper pocket was her wallet with the money she hadn't used during her trip. And strewn around in no particular order were other small items like a pen, chewing gum, perfume, lip balm.

"What are you doing?" Shatha asked from outside the car.

Danah zipped her bag closed. "Sorry Shatha. I was looking for my book to read."

"Read? There's not enough light to read."

Danah slung her handbag over her shoulder. A flashlight. A flashlight would help her read and wouldn't bother any one. Yes! "Wait!" Danah turned back to the car. "I forgot the flashlight." She had seen her Uncle Usama put a small one in the glove compartment.

"What's going on?" Shatha asked.

"Didn't you say there isn't enough light to read? So I'm getting a flashlight."

Fortunately the glove compartment was open. Danah slipped the flashlight into her handbag and closed the car door.

"What are you reading?" Shatha asked.

"*Les Miserable*, have you read it?"

"Years ago, but what a suitable time to read it now."

"I know. Maybe that's why I am so much into the book."

"It's a great book," Shatha said. "Are you reading the complete version or the abridged?"

The bookworm, Danah thought, remembering Amani's name for Shatha. Instead of answering, Danah suddenly turned around and hugged her friend. "I'm so glad I met you Shatha. One day I will tell Amani that you are a great bookworm."

"You're acting strange tonight," Shatha said frowning. But she finally managed a smile as their footsteps scrunched in the loose sand.

CHAPTER ELEVEN

August 22, 1990

BACK INSIDE THE TENT, Danah sat on the floor next to Shatha and her little nieces. Salwa stretched on the ground, her belly bulging out in a big circle. She must have noticed Danah eyeing the box of bottled water next to her.

"Would you like some?" Salwa asked.

"I'd love one," Danah said.

Salwa lifted herself on her elbow. "Here, take two." She handed Danah two plastic bottles.

"Shukran," Danah said. She put one bottle inside her handbag and held on to the other one. "I need to talk to Zainah."

Zainah sat cross-legged with the little baby in her lap. She rocked him to sleep while patting him gently on the shoulder, just as her mother did. She smiled when Danah crouched beside her on the ground.

"Where is your mother?" Danah whispered.

"Outside talking to my father."

"Is he still leaving back to Kuwait?"

"Of course he's still leaving. When my father gives a word he would die to keep it."

"Don't say that," Danah said nervously.

She watched Zainah put her sleeping brother on a blanket, and check on the other children.

"I brought this for your father." Danah lifted the bottle of water in her hand. "He will need it."

"Of course he'll need it."

Danah paused before she whispered. "I have an idea. Let's go put it in his car. He will be pleased to find it later on."

Zainah pranced out of the tent with Danah close behind, Shatha's eyes following them curiously. Outside, Danah carefully studied the path Zainah took toward her father's car. Before reaching it, they heard voices of a man and a woman arguing. Zainah stopped and looked at Danah.

"It's my parents." She pointed at them.

Next to a pick-up truck, Om Thamer, face hidden by her Burga', was pleading with her husband to stay with her and the children.

Danah was about to leave when Zainah said, "Yuba, my friend wants to give you something."

Her father, a thin middle-aged man with long black hair and goatee, signaled his wife to be quiet. His sharp eyes focused on Zainah's hand before he nodded and looked at Danah. "Shukran ya binti, thank you my daughter. I will need that." He took the bottle and slipped it in the side pocket of his brown dishdasha.

"But will you not change your mind for your children's sake?" Om Thamer pleaded again.

Her husband thrust his fingers together in the air as he moved his hand up and down. "I can't. I already gave my word."

Zainah suddenly threw herself at her father and hugged him tightly. "Of course you can't. Please take care of yourself, Yuba," she said tearfully.

Danah examined the pick-up truck closely. In the dark it seemed blue. She peered inside the open trunk with disappointment, it was heaped with bundles of hay and food for animals. When Zainah moved away Danah quickly memorized the license plate-103SF.

Back in the tent, Danah found Shatha telling a story to one of her nieces. The other little girl, her mother and many other women were already asleep. Most of the women around them now were new arrivals. They would eventually leave to Riyadh and other cities in Saudi Arabia, aided by the Saudi government and people. Only a few families, like Shatha's, were staying longer, still hoping to see their families. Soon they too would be urged to leave by the Saudi authorities for security reasons. Danah had heard the men talk about the Iraqi build-up at the borders with Saudi Arabia. President Bush's threat to Saddam brought even more uncertainty about what would happen.

"Are you all right?" Shatha asked.

Danah clutched her handbag. "I'm going outside to read."

"Outside?"

"Yes, remember? I have a flashlight to read with now. I don't want to bother anyone in here."

"You won't bother anyone if you flash the light on your book."

Danah shrugged. "I'd rather read outside in the fresh air." She pulled the silky abaya around her shoulders and stepped away.

"Watch out for scorpions," Shatha said a little louder than necessary.

Goose bumps crept all over Danah's body but she kept on going, watching where she placed her feet. At the entrance she dashed out, bumping into Om Thamer who walked in at the same moment.

"Asfah ya bnaiti, sorry my daughter," Om Thamer said in a nasal voice, touching Danah on the shoulder.

"Ana illi asfah," Danah apologized. She cut to the right and crouched down a few yards from the entrance. Was that Bu Thamer darting toward the men's camp? It was too dark to see anything except for a thin figure moving agilely. The moon seemed to be hiding too, it was nowhere in sight. The stars, millions of them, didn't seem to help illuminate the dark sky.

Had his wife convinced him not to leave after all? Danah nervously opened her bag and pulled out the flashlight aiming it at her wristwatch: eleven. Three more hours. She slowly pointed the light around her looking for scorpions. She remembered the plastic one, the only scorpion she had ever seen, which Amani threw at her when they were children playing in the desert. Danah searched the ground to her left before she edged over, just in case she was sitting on one.

She reached inside her bag for a pen and paper. With a shaking hand she slowly wrote: "Shatha, I'm leaving tonight with Bu Thamer back to Kuwait to my family. I'm hoping he will not find me in his truck until we get safely to where he lives. Please forgive me for not telling you or anyone else. Tell my uncle I hope he forgives me too. Danah."

She checked the time again: eleven thirty. She would wait until one in the morning before leaving the note for Shatha. Then she would go straight to Bu Thamer's truck. She would hide in the back, under the fodder which should provide good cover. She would have to put up with it, even though she had hoped to hide in the back seat of a comfortable car.

Still, if everything went as planned, she might be with her family soon. Her heart throbbed with hope and anxiety.

Suddenly a sound in the distance sent cold shivers through her body. A howling jackal. Danah strained to hear it again, ready to run. But only silence followed. She gathered the abaya around her body even though it must have been eighty degrees.

Twelve midnight. What if Bu Thamer had changed his mind and decided to stay with his family? She had to go on with her plan and wait. If by four in the morning he did not appear, she would just go back to her spot in the tent and get some sleep. She would smell of hay but then she would explain to Shatha about her aborted plan. Later in the day she would be able to take a shower in Riyadh where her uncle wanted to take her. What would she do there in Riyadh? She would wait. That was what every other Kuwaiti outside Kuwait was doing: watch the news and wait. Is that why there was a 'wait' after 'Ku' in the English spelling of Kuwait?

Suddenly Danah jumped to her feet. She must have dozed off. What was the time? She looked at her wristwatch. Too dark to see anything. Oh God. She picked up the flashlight from the ground where she had dropped it and aimed it at her watch: one twenty. Ooof, what a relief. She pulled out the note for Shatha and tip-toed inside the tent.

Luckily, most people were asleep including Shatha. Danah placed the note next to her friend and stealthily dashed out. She shook her abaya from sand and possible scorpions, wrapped it around herself and picked up her bag. Then she headed to the parking lot where Bu Thamer's pick-up waited. Danah flashed the light at the license plate several times before she tossed the bag inside the truck. Next she had to get herself inside, but that wasn't easy. She jumped over the side but the vehicle was higher than she thought. Looking around for something to step on would only waste time. She ran around the truck twice before she figured it out. Throwing her abaya in first, she stepped on the tire while holding on to the metal rim. And then with a swing in the air, she plunged inside, landing with a thud.

After catching her breath, Danah shoved a pile of hay from the left side of the truck. She slumped down in the cleared spot and pulled the hay over her. Then remembering her handbag, she sat up, retrieved it, and repeated the whole procedure again leaving a tiny opening over her nose and mouth.

The smell of dry grass didn't bother Danah as much as the smell of gasoline in a large container not far from her feet. She prayed that Bu Thamer had already filled his tank with gas earlier. Even if he found her he would not harm her, so why was she so nervous?

Thirty minutes later, Danah felt her heart leap to her throat. Without warning, Bu Thamer's door swung open before he jumped inside and closed the door. He started the ignition, backed up in a swift arc, then sped straight forward. Danah held fast to the hay around her, pressing her back against the metal side of the truck.

A couple of times the truck slowed down almost to a stop. Oh no, was he going to stop for inspection at the border? Wouldn't they search the truck? But both times the truck slowly resumed speed. Half an hour later, Bu Thamer was driving so fast that Danah thought they were going to fly.

CHAPTER TWELVE

Inside Kuwait

AT FIRST, DANAH DIDN'T UNDERSTAND THE REASON for the crazy speed with which Bu Thamer drove. She was tossed and banged against the metal sides of the truck. Debris piled over her head, suffocating her. She wished he would slow down a little. But an hour later, when Bu Thamer decreased speed, probably to study the route he had taken, they sank in the sand.

The truck churned and whined under Bu Thamer's attempt to force it out of the loose sand. It got sucked deeper downward while the tires spun ineffectually. Bu Thamer pushed the accelerator lightly but the vehicle only moved sideways as if to find a comfortable position in the sand.

Heat and fumes from the exhaust made Danah dizzy and nauseated. She had to breath in some fresh air. But at that moment Bu Thamer's door opened and slammed shut. A second later he was at her feet.

Danah covered her mouth with both hands to stop herself from throwing up. Would he take her back to the camp?

Bu Thamer moved to the front to get something behind his seat. Then he began working on the tire right under her hiding spot. She could hear his deep rapid breath as he dug in the sand. Was he trying to lift the tire? Or force something under it?

Cold sweat trickled down Danah's face, while her head spun. Was she going to faint? Danah froze as she suddenly felt Bu Thamer's hand touch her foot. She got ready to get pulled out any second. Instead, he removed the gasoline container on which her foot rested. She sighed with relief. The sound of liquid pouring inside the gasoline tank made her crave for water. A minute later Bu Thamer's door opened and shut, and almost exactly at the same time the rear of the truck jerked out and the vehicle took off like a bullet.

Danah threw up uncontrollably. When the convulsions in her stomach stopped, she hauled herself on her back brushing dirt and debris from her face to breath. Now she appreciated the way Bu Thamer had sped along to avoid sinking in the sand. The tires needed to touch the loose sand only lightly otherwise the hollow ground would suck them in easily. One day she would ask him how he managed to get the truck out.

How thirsty she was. A sip from the water bottle in her handbag would wash off the bitter taste of vomit in her mouth. Was it time for her to reveal herself to Bu Thamer? Would he still take her back? She lifted her wrist close to her face and opened just one eye slightly to look at the time. But she was shaking so hard with the movement of the truck she could not see the tiny dials of the watch. Besides, it was still very dark. How could Bu Thamer find his way in the darkness? Bedouin instinct. He must know his way by instinct to be able to avoid the Iraqi army lurking somewhere.

Thinking of the Iraqis made Danah feel sick again. So far,

all she thought of was getting into Kuwait and seeing her family. It had not occurred to her that this meant facing the Iraqis, the invaders. What if they capture Bu Thamer and find her hiding in the truck? What would they do to her? She felt her heartbeat pounding in her ears. She would have to wait and see. She would have to deal with things when they happened instead of worrying about them beforehand as adults do. Still, Danah prayed to God to keep the Iraqis away from her.

Three hours must have passed since the sinking incident, when the truck slowed down again. Oh God please don't let us sink in the sand, Danah prayed earnestly. She lifted her head slightly and opened her eyes. The faint blue color of dawn made her heart flutter with hope. Perhaps it was time to announce her presence to Bu Thamer.

At that very moment the truck came to a complete stop. Danah was just about to sit up and reveal herself when Bu Thamer took off again, this time on a solid road. What a relief. They must be approaching Hadiya, where Bu Thamer lived.

Half an hour later, the truck climbed a little hill, paused on top, then rolled down onto a smoothly paved road. A smile found its way to Danah's face. Next time they stopped, she thought, she would let Bu Thamer know that she had been his traveling companion all along.

That next stop came sooner than Danah expected. Bu Thamer cut the engine and opened his door at the same time. By the time she sat up letting grass and hay tumble down off her head and shoulders, he had already opened the gate of a house, and disappeared inside.

The street was quiet and empty except for a few cars parked in front of the neighbors' houses. So this must be Hadiya, the residential district where Zainah and Farah lived, Danah thought, looking at the small brick house.

She was finally back in Kuwait, her beloved country. She looked up at the blue sky and down at the ground. She loved every inch of it, every grain of sand on the sidewalk. Tears filled her eyes as sadness grew in her heart. Would Zainah and her family ever come back and live in their own house again? Would they be able to sleep in their own beds and play in their own backyard?

Suddenly, Bu Thamer emerged through the gate, and hurried toward his truck. Without looking up he reached for the door handle. That was when Danah called, "Bu Thamer!"

With a sudden jerk of his head, he looked toward the voice, jumping slightly backward upon seeing her. He gaped at Danah who sat smiling inside his truck's flatbed. Slowly a look of recognition showed in his eyes.

"You scared me, may Allah scare your devil," he finally said, but not unkindly.

CHAPTER THIRTEEN

Hadiya

"WHERE DO YOU LIVE?" Bu Thamer asked, sitting down on the floor of his empty living room. He had spread an old newspaper on the floor. On it he placed freshly baked Iranian bread, and a small can of Kraft yellow cheese.

Danah, inhaled the smell of fresh bread before she said, "Khaledeya." Sitting down on the floor she added, "But I don't expect you to take me there."

He gave her a cynical look while handing her one of the round flat breads covered with sesame seeds. "Then how do you plan to get there? Flying? Do you have wings that I don't see?"

Danah's face turned red. "Please don't laugh at me. I'm sorry I sneaked in your truck. All I wanted was to be with my family. Just as much as Zainah and her mother wanted you to stay with them."

Bu Thamer didn't reply. He stood up, darted out of the living room and came back with a can opener and a fresh pot of tea. He opened the can on both sides, then pushed one of the lids inside the can until the cheese slid out from the other side. He cut the block in two halves, gave her one, and began eating his share with bread.

"I will walk to my house," she said with determination.

Bu Thamer gave her a sharp look before he took a sip of tea, making a lot of noise slurping it. "Do you know how far we are from Khaledeya?"

Danah shook her head. She never heard of Hadiya before until Zainah told her about it. Tears gathered in her eyes, she looked down at her food so that Bu Thamer would not see them.

"Listen," Bu Thamer said gently. "When I saw you in my truck earlier I was determined to take you to your family no matter where you lived. But one of my neighbors just told me that the Iraqis have ordered all Kuwaitis to change their license plates to Iraqi plates. They will severely punish anyone who still drives with a Kuwaiti license plate."

Danah held back her tears. "I told you, you are not responsible for me. I don't want you to have any problems because of me."

Deep in thought, Bu Thamer didn't answer. "Mishref," he suddenly exclaimed. "I can drive you there through back roads instead of taking the Sixth Ring Road which will be infested with Iraqi soldiers. Do you have any relatives in Mishref? You can stay with them until they find a way to take you to your family."

Danah thought hard but no one came to mind. She had some friends there but she didn't know their address. She glanced at the time on her wrist, almost eight in the morning. How she wished she could let her family know she was in Kuwait. Perhaps they could come and get her.

"Telephone!" She jumped up to her feet. "Bu Thamer, do you have a telephone? You must have a telephone. I heard the

Iraqis left local telephone lines running." Her eyes searched around the bare room.

Before he pointed at it, Danah saw the device on the floor in one of the corners and pranced to it. She picked it up, put the receiver against her ear and started laughing. "It works, it works." She dialed the number she knew so well. A busy signal came through. She sat down on the floor and tried again a dozen times. Each time the same thing happened. She finally put the receiver down and looked toward Bu Thamer who was clearing away the breakfast things.

"It's busy," she said, trying one more time.

"Only one solution remains," Bu Thamer said. "I will drive you to Mishref and from there I'll walk you to Khaledeya."

Danah's heart sank. She knew the distance between Khaledeya and Mishref was not within walking distance. Besides, she hadn't sneaked into Kuwait to be a burden on this nice man. "No," she said. "That means you will have to leave your truck unattended. If the Iraqis see it they will definitely take it."

Bu Thamer's face darkened. He must have agreed with her. "So what do you want to do then?"

"I don't know. Let me keep trying to call my family."

"I will be outside in the yard." He dashed out of the living room.

Danah held her breath while she dialed again, but the same busy signal sounded in her ears. After the tenth time she gave up and walked outside to the front yard.

The heat from the unveiled bright sun made Danah's jeans feel like hot leather on her legs. She rolled up the sleeves of her brown blouse, and straightened her hair in a short pony tail with pins she found in the bathroom when she washed earlier. They must have belonged to Zainah, she thought recalling the girl's long wavy hair.

Bu Thamer was nowhere in sight. Perhaps he was in the backyard. A tiled narrow pathway between the house and fence connected the front yard to the back. It was a small backyard mainly used as a coop for chickens and birds, but there were none at the moment. Danah gazed at the remains of food, feathers and dirt, and wondered if the Iraqi soldiers ate the chickens like they did the birds and animals in the Zoo. She remembered how that piece of news had infuriated Julie. "That shows what kind of army Saddam has," she had said with anger.

Danah continued to the other side of the backyard. Old and broken chairs and toys where piled in a small heap. She briefly scanned them thinking of Farah, then turned around into the pathway back to the front yard, when her mind registered something. She stopped. Rushing back to the pile she now saw it with her own eyes. Leaning against the chicken wire fence was a three speed bicycle. It was a little smaller than the one she rode in New York, and it had a basket on the handle bars. Thamer must have used it to get groceries for his mother. She pulled the bike backward toward her and squeezed the hand brakes to test them. They squeaked loudly but they worked.

Danah laughed out loud with joy. She got on the bicycle through the narrow sidewalk to the front yard. "Bu Thamer! Bu Thamer!" she yelled excitedly as she spun around and around.

With a pale face, Bu Thamer rushed into the yard from the street. He stopped when he saw Danah on the bike. "You scared me again, may Allah scare your devil."

"This is it, Bu Thamer. This is the solution."

"What? What?" He tugged at the hairs of his goatee.

"I will ride the bike from Mishref to Khaledeya. It will take me less than two hours."

The man shook his head from side to side as if he were trying to pour sand out of his ears. "A girl? A girl rides a bike in the street? And when? When the animals, the Iraqi soldiers, are in the street watching? No, no, no. You cannot do that."

"Yes I can!" Danah said firmly, getting off the bike. "They won't know that I'm a girl. Just wait a second." She rested the bike on the iron gate and ran to Bu Thamer's pick up truck. From the back she snatched her handbag, opened it and took out the cap that Julie had given her. She placed the cap on her head, rolled down her sleeves, and got on the bike again.

Leaning forward, her face hidden between her shoulders, Danah rode the bike to the street in front of Bu Thamer. "What do you think?" She turned back toward him. "Do you think anyone will realize I'm a girl?"

A big grin spread on Bu Thamer's face. "Maybe not. Maybe not. So come, let me pump some air into those tires."

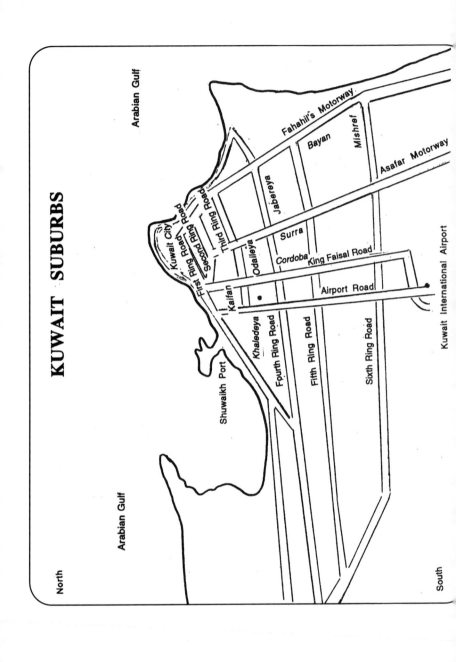

KUWAIT SUBURBS

CHAPTER FOURTEEN

Kuwait City

"GO NORTH THROUGH BAYAN, keeping this motorway to your right," Bu Thamer said, pointing at Fahahil's Motorway. He had stopped his truck at the roundabout that connected the northern and southern sections of Mishref. That was the farthest he could venture without being noticed by the Iraqis.

He lifted his son's bicycle from the back of the truck and rolled it toward Danah. "Once you are out of Bayan," he continued, "Carefully cross under the bridge and turn left to Jabereya. From there keep riding west and you will be in Surra then Cordoba."

"That's good, from there I can find my way." Danah jumped up and down with excitement. "I have an aunt who lives there. Thank you so much Bu Thamer," she said shaking his hand. "May Allah give you health and strength." She grinned, she sounded just like her father.

"Don't forget your abaya and handbag." Bu Thamer handed them to her.

Danah placed the handbag in the bicycle basket and gave him the abaya. "I don't need it anymore." She got on the bike and placed her right foot on the pedal.

"Would you be careful my daughter?" Bu Thamer said, worry and concern showing in his eyes.

"Don't worry Bu Thamer," Danah said getting ready to ride away. "Please give my regards to Om Thamer and Zainah."

He nodded and watched her ride on the sandy sidewalk.

"And Bu Thamer," she swung around toward him. "Don't promise any more neighbors to come back for them, wallah."

He smiled sadly and waved goodbye. She slid down the sandy curb to the paved road and sped up looking back only once to see Bu Thamer's truck back up and drive away.

At nine in the morning, the roads in Bayan were almost deserted. Every once in a while a car would pass. Except for two or three Indian men, probably servants in some of the houses, there were no other pedestrians in the streets. Piles of garbage left on the sidewalks here and there filled the air with a foul stench.

On the bridge to Jabereya, Danah had a full view of the Fahahil's Fast Motorway. That was when facing the enemy became a reality. Goose bumps crawled on her skin like a scorpion scuttling across sand. There they were: uniformed soldiers in their tanks and jeeps. Danah looked away. Sweat from the searing heat of the sun mingled with cold sweat. She had to keep her head down between her shoulders. They had to think she was a boy. She rode on hunched over, worry hanging like a sack of sand over her shoulders.

In Jabereya signs of life appeared. Men and children walked up and down the main street. The pharmacy that she had once visited with her mother was crowded with people. Next door a bookstore displayed newspapers and magazines on racks outside on the sidewalk. Danah was relieved that no one seemed to pay attention to her as she passed them on the bike.

Before taking the small bridge which connected Jabereya to the district of Surra, Danah paused to rest. She remembered how the bridge curved up a little hill before it led down to Surra. Being so tired and thirsty she would not be able to ride over it without taking a sip of water.

Danah got off her bike, and pulled it over the wide sandy sidewalk, a little distance away from the busy main street. There wasn't a single tree to rest under. She snapped open the plastic cap of the bottled water, the one that Salwa had given her just the night before, and poured warm liquid down her parched throat. The rest she splashed over her face and neck.

Just before starting up the hill, the roar of an engine sounded from close behind. Danah turned around, and found herself staring into the face of an Iraqi soldier. His face was dark and grim. He held a machine gun as he sat next to the driver. Danah's hand lost its grip of the bike which dropped down to the ground. She bent down to pick it up and avoid looking at the soldiers crowded in the back of the truck. They drove past laughing and sneering.

"Kuwaitis can't even ride a bike?" one of them mocked in Iraqi Arabic. The rest laughed even louder.

Relieved to see the truck gone, Danah waited several minutes before she pushed the bike to the top of the hill.

"Kuwaitis can't even ride a bike," she mimicked angrily. She then got on the bike and glided down the hill toward the flat road of Surra. "We'll show you what Kuwaitis can do," she threatened, swinging her fist in the air. The bicycle wobbled. One day she'd have to learn how to ride the bike with one hand, she promised feeling foolish.

Riding through the residential district of Surra took no more than ten minutes. At Damascus Avenue, which intersected Surra and Cordoba, Danah decided to divert from the route that Bu Thamer planned for her. Instead of crossing to Cordoba, she would take Damascus Avenue north, to the Fourth Ring road. Then she would turn west passing Odaileya and straight to Khaledeya. That should be much shorter and faster, she thought, imagining herself in her mother's arms.

At the intersection of Damascus Avenue and the Fourth Ring road Danah realized the wisdom of Bu Thamer's plan. By taking quiet residential roads, she would have avoided possible encounter with the enemy and heavy traffic.

The smooth Fourth Ring Road that she had once known, was now destroyed. Pieces of asphalt jutted out and scattered all over the road, making it difficult to ride in a straight line. Civilian cars, burnt and damaged, lay abandoned on both sides of the street like dead animal carcasses. Tanks and military armor rolled by digging deeper into the road. Street signs had been scribbled over with black paint. Cars with Iraqi license plates honked and nearly pushed her off the road as they passed by.

Danah couldn't control her tears. "Why? Why?" she repeated as she looked at the devastation. Suddenly, a big slab of asphalt jutted out of the right side of the road. To avoid it she swerved to the middle of the street. A speeding car honked madly as the driver tried to avoid hitting her. Danah squeezed the brakes hard and hit the broken asphalt to the right. Next thing she knew, she was flying in the air headlong before crashing to the ground.

Shocked, Danah remained motionless in the dirt, face down for a long time. A burning sensation spread on her forehead and chin. Would she be able to move? She struggled to her feet feeling the aches and pains in every part of her body. She found the Disney cap on the ground and adjusted it back on her head.

"Are you all right my son?" somebody called in Kuwaiti Arabic from a car.

"Yes, yes, thank you," Danah answered feebly.

When the car moved on, she hauled the bike up to see if the wheels were still straight. Luckily, they weren't too bent up. Painfully, Danah dragged her bike to the street. She looked toward University Bridge when her apprehension turned to a rock in the pit of her stomach. On top of that bridge, on both sides of the road, two military vehicles perched like small fortresses. Soldiers moved slowly back and forth monitoring the road underneath the bridge. Or was it the university across the street from her home that they were watching?

Danah stopped to think for a moment. It would be foolish to cross the bridge between the two military vehicles. The only other alternative was to take the Third Ring Road. Turning left on the Third Ring Road should put her on the main street of Khaledeya.

Mounting her bike again, Danah managed to make the turn. To her left, Kuwait University campus stretched between the Fourth and Third Ring Roads. When she drew parallel to the main gate, it took some effort to turn her head and look at the dear familiar buildings. Anger, horror and hatred swept over her all at the same time. Instead of the Kuwaiti flags at the gate, there now flew two Iraqi flags over a huge picture of Saddam, smiling in a military uniform. The fence around the campus was barricaded with military tanks. Black soot covered the once white buildings of the university.

If there were military vehicles on the other side of campus, then she could not enter her house through the front gate. Now she'd have to ride to the back street and enter through the rear gate. Her heart pounded violently. What if the Iraqis had taken over all the houses facing campus? What if her family...

Danah shook her head to force the thoughts from her mind. She wiped her forehead, looked at her hand and saw a trickle of blood on her palm.

Adjusting the cap over the cut, she pedaled on holding the handle bars with her left hand. Minutes later she realized what she had just done. She was riding with one hand! So she finally did it, she thought, without the thrill she would have felt in Central Park. Still, she did it, she thought again, turning west on the Third Ring road.

Instead of taking the main street of Khaledeya and turning toward the back of her house, Danah cut through a yard leading to the back street. She knew every corner, every inch of that block. The tiny street just ahead would lead to the cul de sac at the back of her own house. And there was the green checker board brick house that she had always thought looked funny. Now it looked beautiful. She gazed at it with tearful eyes as she rode around it to the street she had grown up on.

How desolate and abandoned the street seemed. Smoke from a pile of garbage filled the air with a stench of burnt food and refuse. But, worst of all, Bu Salem's house, the house of her childhood friend, Ashwaq, was burnt down. Totally burnt. Only a few blackened beams remained standing like lone monuments.

Danah stopped in front of the house and wept. She cried out loud: "Please God, don't make this real, please!" Her shoulders quivered, her body trembled. She covered her face with both hands, hoping that when she removed them the nightmare would be over and Bu Salem's house would stand there as it had since she was born.

For several minutes, Danah stood there crying. She did not dare look toward her house, three houses down. She gradually became aware of someone at her back, tapping lightly on her shoulder. When the hand grasped her arm she jumped back expecting to see an Iraqi soldier.

"What's wrong with you?" a woman asked in broken Arabic. "Why you crying?"

"Bimla?" Danah exclaimed. "Bimla!" She hugged the woman who worked at her house since she was a little girl.

Bimla pushed Danah away. "Who are you, walad?"

Danah chuckled. The woman was addressing her as a boy. "Bimla, it's me Danah." She almost took her cap off and let her hair down but that might still be risky.

"Danah not here, she's in America," Bimla insisted.

"Is the door open?" Danah asked, riding toward her house. It was still there, her eyes gazed at the familiar building. It was still there. "Alhamdu Lillah, thank God," Danah said sighing deeply. "Alhamdu Lillah."

The iron gate stood open. Danah pedaled inside the yard, stopped in front of the main door, dropped the bike on the tiled floor, and rushed inside the house.

CHAPTER FIFTEEN

August 23, 1990

A COLD SHUDDER WENT THROUGH Danah when she stepped inside her family's house. She searched the rooms on the first floor, but no one was there. The house was deathly quiet.

"Yumma!!!" she screamed from the top of the staircase, her legs struggling to steady her. When no answer came, tears gathered in her eyes. She grabbed the banister to keep from falling, and began sobbing. Was this what she had come for? To find an empty house? To find her family gone? Where could she find them now? Where could they be? Were they still alive? "Yumma!!" she cried again with pain.

"Bimla? Is that you?" a voice came from the basement.

Not believing her ears, Danah stopped sobbing and listened.

"Bimla?" her mother's voice sounded again.

"Yumma!" Danah yelped, jumping to her feet and skipping the steps to the basement. Her mother at the bottom of the stairway, looked like a skeleton, her mouth wide open, her face ghostly pale, she stared at Danah in disbelief.

Danah threw herself on her mother, hugging and kissing her. "Yumma, I'm so happy to see you."

Still in disbelief, her mother took Danah by the shoulders and pushed her gently away to look in her face. Danah removed the cap from her head and smiled through her tears. "Don't you know me anymore?"

Her mother pulled her back to her chest and hugged her for a long time, the way Danah had dreamed of, since the second of August.

"Yumma? Who is this?" Amani stood behind them, and repeated the question many times before her mother finally released Danah.

"Danah!" Amani yelled with joy. She hugged her sister while giggling and laughing. "Danah, I can't believe it. I can't believe it. But what are these bruises on your face?"

"What's all this noise?" Her father walked out of a room at the far end of the basement.

At first Danah couldn't recognize him. Besides the gray beard which he never had before, his hair had turned white. His face was haggard and sallow. Danah pounced to meet him. She kissed his cheeks and felt the bristles of his beard against her sore face.

"Where is Aziz?" Danah asked, and looked around the dark basement.

"He spends most of the time with Talal," Amani answered. "But how did you get here? I'm still finding it hard to believe you're real."

Bimla, who stopped in the middle of the stairway, watched as if she was looking at a ghost. "I saw her first," she finally said.

Danah laughed sitting next to her mother on the couch. "Did you lock the door, Bimla?" her mother asked.

"Yes, of course," Bimla said in English. She came down the stairway and sat on the floor near them.

"Danah!" her father said. "You have to tell us right now how you got here, and why is your face bruised like this?"

Amani sat next to Bimla on the floor. "I hope you didn't collaborate with the enemy to get here."

"No way," Danah said. She then began telling her story starting at the day Shatha called her at Uncle Faisal's house, telling her she was going to Saudi Arabia.

When Danah got to the point where she hid in Bu Thamer's truck her father shook his head disapprovingly, while her mother held her own face with both hands.

"How could you do such a thing?" she asked.

"Well, that was the only way to get here," Danah said giggling.

"That wasn't a wise thing to do," her father said. "And did Bu Thamer bring you here? Where is he? We should thank him."

Before Danah could answer, Bimla said, "She came on a bike."

"What?" her father yelled.

Danah explained while her mother wrung her hands tightly. "You could have been killed," she moaned.

"But I'm right here with you now, am I not?" Danah said.

"You were just lucky." Amani laughed.

"Didn't you say I should be here to attend your wedding? Here I am, two weeks before your wedding."

The smile vanished from Amani's face. "What wedding?"

Danah gazed at the faces around her, they all looked haggard, tired, and much thinner than when she had left. "What do you mean?"

"Talal and I decided to get married on the day the Iraqis leave our country."

"Oh good, I thought you two decided you didn't like each other anymore."

Amani lightly slapped Danah's knee.

"Danah!" Father said. "Thank God for your safety, but what you did was not smart at all. You endangered your life for no reason."

Her mother nodded in agreement. "I was happy you were safe away from this hell we are living in."

Danah hugged her mother. "To live in this hell with you, is better than being in heaven without you." Her mother hugged her again and cried.

"Yumma, there is no reason to cry now. I'm sure Danah needs to take a shower and have something to eat. I'll make her a sandwich."

"That's true," Danah said, giving her mother a quick kiss on the cheek. She climbed up the stairway. "I'll be back to tell you all about Uncle Faisal and Julie."

At the door of her room Danah was suddenly overwhelmed by a strange feeling. The feeling of entering the past, the room of her childhood. Even though it had only been three weeks since she left, it felt like she had grown up so many years since then. The little girl that whined and complained about nothing and everything was no more. A different girl had returned to take her place. Her family seemed tired and needed some cheer and she would do anything to help and take care of them.

After a long shower and a change of clothes, Danah went to the kitchen where Amani prepared a sandwich with cheese. "Everything we eat is from cans these days," Amani said pushing the plate toward Danah on the kitchen table. "And there isn't much left of that either."

Danah sat down and gazed at Amani's beautiful thin face. "You mean we might run out of food?"

Amani nodded looking at Danah's flat chest. "And you already look like skin and bones. Didn't they feed you in America?"

Danah swallowed the first bite she took out of the sandwich. "What happened to Bu Salem's family?"

Amani nervously tapped her fingers on the table. "I was hoping you wouldn't ask."

"Tell me." Danah's heart began throbbing with fear.

"On the first day of the invasion, Salem and his father sent the women away to stay with relatives. They both stayed in the house along with some of their friends. They watched the Iraqi soldiers on campus from their windows until one day at dawn we heard gun shots. When we looked out, we saw the Iraqis drag Salem and his father out, hands tied behind their backs. Before they took them away in their trucks they burnt their house down right in front of their eyes. Nobody has seen them since."

Danah choked on her tears. Oh God, she moaned, how could such a horrible thing happen to such nice people? Bu Salem's kind face smiling at her was so clear in her mind. She tried hard not to imagine what Amani just told her.

"What about you?" Danah asked after a while. "Do they leave you alone?"

"No. They come here every week and search our house."

Danah winced. "What right do they have?" Then she realized how silly her question was. "What do you do when they do that?"

"Father walks around with them. Mother and I cover ourselves with our abayas and stay out of their way."

"What about Aziz?"

"Since that incident at Bu Salem's house, father asked him to keep a low profile. He now spends most of his time with Talal in Bayan."

"What do they do?"

"They…" Amani hesitated. But her face suddenly smiled as she nodded toward the kitchen door saying, "There is Aziz."

Excitedly, Danah stood up knocking back her chair. She leapt toward her brother and hugged him. "I'm so glad you're safe," she said when she let go of him.

"How did you get here?" Aziz asked, his round face full of surprise.

"It's a long story."

Aziz pulled a chair and sat down. "I want to hear it now." He looked thin in the blue t-shirt and jeans he wore. He hadn't shaved in several days.

"Since when do you wear jeans in Kuwait?" Danah wanted to tease him like she used to in the 'good old days'.

Amani answered, "The Kuwaiti dishdasha seems to draw the Iraqis' attention. In the jeans, they would think he's Palestinian or some other Arabic nationality."

"Come on Danah," Aziz said impatiently. "Tell me how you entered Kuwait."

Danah told him the story just as she had her parents. "And here I am," she said at the end.

"How much military do they have in the districts you passed through to get here?" Aziz asked.

"I used back streets where there is hardly any military. But I saw many of them on Fahahil's Motorway, Fourth Ring road, and of course here on campus."

"The bastards are using our campus as a center for communications. Some of their top officials practically live here."

"Aziz, Alhamdu Lillah you're here." Mother stood at the door. "Talal just called to ask about you, and I began to worry."

Aziz stood up and kissed his mother's forehead.

"The phone is working?" Danah asked Amani.

"Yes, thank goodness."

"So why was it busy all morning when I tried to call you?"

Amani furtively looked at her mother before she whispered to Danah, "I'll tell you later."

"Danah," mother said. "We are waiting for you downstairs to tell us about your visit with your uncle and his wife. Amani let's make tea and…"

Just at that moment an explosion sounded so loud it shook the floor under their feet. Rumblings and more explosions followed. Danah froze in her spot. She watched her mother, Amani and Aziz run toward the stairway leading to the basement.

"Run Danah, don't just stand there," her mother said in an agitated voice. She rushed back to her daughter, grabbed her by the arm, and led her downstairs.

Her father, who was already in the basement, sat cross-legged on the floor. He held the holy book of the Koran and read aloud shaking his body with every word he read. The rumblings continued while her family gathered around her father, their lips moving silently. Danah held her mother's cold hands, trying to warm them in hers.

Bimla sat just a few feet away from them crying out loud.

"They are blasting the police station in Kaifan," Aziz said, his face as white as the dishdasha he no longer wore. "That's why it sounds that close."

"How do you know?" Danah asked.

Amani gave her a quick look before she addressed Bimla, "Stop crying now, will you?"

Later that night, when her mother and father retreated

into the back room in the basement to sleep, Danah unfolded a mattress for herself next to Amani's in one corner of the basement. Bimla was already asleep in the opposite corner. All lights were off except for the one at the top of the staircase, where her father checked the door lock for the tenth time before he finally went to sleep.

Danah lay on her back listening to Bimla's rhythmic snoring. Every few minutes the humming of the electric generator would resume after a brief pause, muffling other noises coming from outside the house.

"Amani! Are you asleep?" Danah whispered.

"No."

"You promised to tell me why the phone was busy all morning when I tried to call you."

A long moment of silence followed before Amani answered. Her voice came very low, and in the darkness it sounded strange. "Talal and Aziz are working with the resistance. During the night they fax me announcements and directions for their group along with a list of names to fax and e-mail. Early in the morning, I read their directions and fax the announcements and e-mail them through the computer. That keeps the phone line busy."

Danah's heart sank, cold perspiration gathering on her forehead. Something, like a huge black monster, began gnawing at both her sides in the darkness. She imagined Salem and his father next door pushed out of their house by the Iraqi soldiers. Tears silently flowed down the sides of her face.

"You must not mention it to mother or father," came Amani's voice again, calm and confident. "It's better if they don't know."

CHAPTER SIXTEEN

August 24, 1990

*E*ARLY NEXT MORNING Danah felt Amani shift in her bed before she quietly rose up and climbed the steps to the main floor. She followed her noiselessly to Aziz's room. Amani tore off the rolled paper on top of the fax machine and began reading.

"Can I see the notes?" Danah whispered.

Without turning around, Amani held the papers in front of Danah to read along. The first message said:

"Amani, the message on page B should be sent tonight to the following numbers only. Do not send anywhere else.

It's important that you follow these directions very carefully."

Danah glanced at the numbers the message contained. There were only four, all began with the digits 52 which meant the owners lived in the southern districts.

"Let's see the message they want you to fax tonight," Danah asked.

Amani rolled open the page. It was brief:

'Pick new shipment of candy from the same location as last

time. Please share with the other three parties equally. Be careful. Good luck!!'

"Candy?" Danah exclaimed loudly.

"Ssh!" Amani turned a grim face toward Danah. She hesitated before she finally whispered, "It's the word they use for weapons."

Danah gasped. At that moment their mother opened the door. "What are you girls doing in your brother's room?"

"Not much Yumma," Amani answered casually. "I was showing Danah Aziz's computer. "

"Come have breakfast first," her mother said, and turned toward the kitchen.

"Weapons?" Danah whispered still alarmed. "Talal and Aziz should not be dealing with weapons."

"Let's just pray for their safety, Danah," Amani said quietly after folding the fax paper and hiding it in her gown pocket. She walked with Danah out of Aziz's room. "There is nothing else we can do," she added as she climbed up the stairway to her room.

In the kitchen her mother and father silently dunked bread in their cups of tea with milk. Danah joined them. How could Amani be so calm and composed? How could she let Aziz and Talal do such a dangerous thing without discouraging them? How could she refrain from telling her parents about such a dangerous thing?

"Yuba?" Danah addressed her father. "Why are people burning garbage in the streets?"

"What else can they do? There is no garbage pick up any more." He pushed his cup away and stood up. "I'm going to the mosque for Friday's prayers," he announced before he left the kitchen.

"Has he left the house since the invasion?" Danah asked her mother.

"Just on Fridays to the mosque, and once or twice to the co-op next door." Her mother passively stirred sugar in her second cup of tea with the tiny spoon. She then looked at Danah with worried eyes and asked, "What would you have done if you came back and nobody was here?"

"Are you still thinking about that?"

"It just occurred to me that if we had left like many other people, what would you have done?"

"Knowing my father, I knew he would never leave the house, let alone the country," Danah said smiling. "Why do grown ups worry about things that don't happen?"

As if talking to herself, her mother said, "Tomorrow morning they will come again, searching for weapons or Americans. They don't leave us alone because of the location. I told your father many times it would be better if we stayed with his aunt in Cordoba, she's old and all by herself, but he won't listen."

Danah chewed on the inside of her lower lip and gazed at her mother's dark face. What would she do if she was aware of what Aziz was involved in? Did she have a mother's intuition that he was up to something? Was that why she worried constantly?

"I'm going upstairs to my room." Danah stood up. "Do you need anything?"

"Bimla and I are going to pick the dates from the palm tree. You can help us bring them in later. The Iraqi soldiers were eyeing them last time they were here."

"In Sha' Allah, Yumma. I'll be back in a few minutes to help," Danah said before leaving the kitchen table.

The windows in her room must not have been opened since she had left, Danah thought as she drew the curtains open. Fresh air would be a good idea on Friday, since her family told her that the Iraqi military suspended their bomb attacks on the holy day. How can Muslims harm other Muslims or any other humans for that matter? How can they justify their actions? Is there any rightful reason for killing and harming other people?

No. Danah shook her head as she stood in front of the window. Hot air rushed into the cool room brushing the side of her cold face. She took a deep deep breath, but the burden that sat on her chest since the first day of the invasion kept growing heavier by the minute. She fought the tears that began forming in her eyes as they focused on the campus facing her room. The campus that she had always assumed would be there when she graduated from high school.

"My university," she used to call it.

"It's Aziz's university now," Amani used to tease her when Aziz enrolled three years earlier. He would've had only one year before he graduated from the computer science department.

Danah looked at the empty sand parking lot that used to be so crowded with student cars. She used to watch them every morning before she went to her school, competing over spots. Since there wasn't enough parking area inside campus, students used to park in front of their house and the neighbors', blocking their way out. Some neighbors put up 'Do Not Park' signs, but when a student was late to a class, he or she didn't pay much attention to such a sign.

Danah sighed again. Those were the happy days, she thought. Would they ever come back?

"Allahu Akbar, God is great," called the Muethen from the mosque nearby. The first two words of the call for prayers. Danah repeated the words as a good omen in answer to her question. Yes, those care free days would return, for God is greater than the Iraqi army.

Feeling a little better Danah decided to change clothes and go help her mother gather the dates from the palm tree in the front yard.

She reached to the top of the sliding window and pushed down hard to hook the latch to the lock. As she did that her eyes caught a glimpse of something or someone running toward her house while trying to hide under the fence of the neighbor's house. Danah inched to the left side of the window and peered hard at the moving figure that hid under a tree.

From the main entrance of the university a military jeep with two Iraqi soldiers dashed out like a bull then halted in the middle of the two-way street. The soldier in the passenger's seat pointed down at the road facing Danah's window, while the driver revved up the engine before moving down that direction.

At the sound of the engine, the figure suddenly took off and darted down the alley. Danah let out a yell that came out as a squeak. It was Aziz, her only brother Aziz.

Taking to her heels, Danah was down the stairway in two big jumps, and out in the front yard in three giant strides. She opened the gate and galloped in the direction where her brother was running.

"Aziz!" she called once. He sprinted out, white as a ghost. "Quick, the gate is open." They both ran inside the yard. "Go to my room," she said, closing the iron gate behind them.

"What is it?" Her mother appeared in the corridor which connected the front yard to the back yard.

"Yumma, it's nothing go back please," Danah said, trying to sound calm.

"Was that Aziz?" She followed Danah inside the house.

"Yes, he wants me to give him something," Danah said before she ran to her room. Closing the door, she stood face to face with Aziz. He wore blue jeans and a white t-shirt and shook like a leaf. "Wait here, I'm going downstairs to bring one of your dishdashas from your room."

Danah scurried down the stairway to Aziz's room, pulled a dishdasha off the hanger behind the door and climbed up the stairs back to her room in one minute.

"Put this on quickly." She gave it to Aziz. Opening her closet, she pulled out a white t-shirt and a pair of blue jeans, and quickly slipped them on. She then took hers and Aziz's discarded clothes and threw them in the laundry basket behind her door. From the top of the chest of drawers Danah grabbed the Disney cap that Julie gave her, twisted her hair up and placed the cap on top of it.

"What are you doing?" Aziz asked nervously.

Before Danah answered, the bell of the front gate echoed in the quiet house, followed by the banging of the metal doors. Danah swallowed hard to wet her dry throat. "Is there anywhere you can hide?"

"Hide? I'm not going to hide," he said, opening the door of her room.

Danah grabbed his arm. "Wait, just stay out of the way, please. Go to our parents' room, wait there." She shoved him gently toward her parents' room, then she casually descended the staircase.

The voices outside in the front yard grew louder before the door facing the staircase was thrown open and the two Iraqi soldiers darted in followed by Bimla and her mother.

"Are you looking for me?" Danah asked, not recognizing her own voice.

The two men stared at Danah with fierce eyes. They were both short, dark and unkempt.

"Where were you just a few minutes ago?" One of them

who seemed a little older than the other asked in Arabic with a strong Iraqi accent.

"Walking around my university, is there something wrong with that?"

"You can be killed for that," the younger soldier threatened.

"Your ambassador in the United States said you would never do such a thing," Danah said in that strange voice as she took the last step down the staircase. On the table in the living room *The New York Times* she brought with her was spread open since she showed it to Amani the day before. She picked it up and thrust the paper in front of their faces, her Disney cap falling on the floor.

"Read it," she said. "Don't you Iraqis read English? Your ambassador claims that you soldiers are not harming anyone in Kuwait, and anything otherwise is just a big lie." Danah eyed them, as she prayed to God that they did not read English — since none of what she said was written in the paper. She was only repeating the words of the Iraqi man she talked to over the phone in New York.

"Please!" her father, who just rushed in, begged, "Please don't listen to her, she's only a child."

The older soldier looked at the father. "Is this your daughter?"

"Yes, and she's only a child."

The younger soldier who was looking closely at a picture in the American newspaper folded it and threw it on the floor. "She was trying to get inside the university, and that's a big crime."

Her father tapped on his chest. "I am responsible of her behavior and I apologize. I will not let that happen again."

The older soldier nodded. "Is the black Mercedes parked outside yours?"

"Yes."

"Do you have the keys to it?"

"Yes I do." Danah's father reached for the keys in his dish-dasha's side pocket.

"You have no right to take our car," Danah yelled.

"Danah be quiet," her father scolded her angrily.

Then handing the soldiers the keys he said, "Take it, it's yours."

With a grin on his face, the soldier took the keys. "Make sure you keep your daughter away from the university area." He then turned around to leave with his comrade.

Danah shouted, "It is our country and our university, you're the ones who should stay away from it!"

The older soldier turned around. "Behave yourself girl. If this kind man wasn't your father we would have taken you away by now."

"She's just an ignorant child," her father repeated following them outside.

Danah was about to follow them out when she heard her mother utter a strange sound followed by a scream from Bimla. "What is it?" Danah asked. But she needed no answer, Bimla was holding her mother who dangled in her arms like a rag doll.

"Bring a glass of cold water quick," Danah said to Bimla taking her mother in her arms.

"Yumma, please wake up, yumma!" She patted her mother gently on the cheek.

Bimla came back with a glass of water. She poured some of it on her hand and washed Om Aziz's face. Danah lifted her mother's head and tried to pour some water in her mouth. Her mother's face moved slightly while her lips trembled.

"Yumma are you all right? Please take a sip of water."

Instead of taking the water her mother pushed the glass

away, hugged Danah to her, and wept out loud. She kept uttering incomprehensible words while sobbing like a child. Danah and Bimla joined her in crying.

"Danah!" her father shouted angrily at the door. "Where is that irresponsible girl?" He stormed into the hallway.

Danah let go of her mother, wiped her tears with the sleeve of her t-shirt and got ready to face her angry father. At that moment Aziz and Amani scrambled down the stairway from upstairs.

"Yuba," Aziz said addressing his father.

"Aziz?" father said with surprise. "I didn't know you were here? You should have seen how this ignorant sister of yours talked to the Iraqi soldiers. She shouldn't have come back from where she was. She should have…"

Aziz stepped forward toward his father putting his hand on his shoulder. "It's all right Yuba, calm down please. Danah has just saved my life."

CHAPTER SEVENTEEN

Leaving Khaledeya

DANAH SAT QUIETLY IN THE BACK SEAT with her mother, Amani and Bimla. In the front seat was her father and Aziz next to Talal who was driving his own car. It was almost ten at night, no stars in the moonless sky, and no one had said a word for the last fifteen minutes since they left their house in Khaledeya.

Danah stared at the back of Talal's head in front of her, wrapped in his white ghitra. He hadn't said much since he drove into their yard through the main gate which Aziz opened for him about an hour earlier. Bimla and her mother carried boxes filled with canned and dried food to the trunk of the car, while she and Amani carried the handbags packed with clothing.

"Don't take much now," her father had said. "We'll come back for more clothes in a few days."

Poor father, Danah thought moving uncomfortably in the back seat. He almost went crazy when Aziz explained the real reason why the Iraqis came to their house. He moved his eyes

107

from face to face and then pointed at Danah with his trembling finger, shaking his head. What did he want to say? She hadn't waited to hear it, she rose from her chair and hugged him.

After patting her on the shoulder several times, father announced in a weak voice. "We have to leave the house right away."

"Why?" Danah asked.

Father sat down next to Amani and mother. "The Iraqis will watch us closely from now on. All our lives are in danger. We're going to stay with my aunt in Cordoba as your mother wishes."

A sigh of relief escaped her mother's lips. Danah looked at Aziz. "Is your car here?"

"No," he shook his head. He addressed father. "I can call Talal and have him pick us up." When father agreed Aziz asked, "What time should we leave?"

"As late as possible. That will give us time to pack and lock up everything, and hopefully leave at night without them seeing us."

Everybody got busy after that. Following her father's orders, Danah added only a few items to her handbag which she hadn't unpacked yet. When they all got in the car she placed her handbag on her lap and looked at Thamer's bicycle left under the henna tree in the back yard. She wished she could take it with, but she knew there was no room for such a thing.

Outside the window to her left, the roads, completely deserted, seemed darker than usual. She looked up at the street lights that used to illuminate every street in the city. They were broken or in most cases missing. Was it possible that the Iraqis took them as well? She heard about the looting of electronics and other equipment, but street lights?

She glanced at Amani sitting to her right. From the time they had driven off, Amani's eyes froze on her hands, clasped tightly in her lap. Once in a while her left fingers played with the engagement ring, on her right forefinger which once glimmered with diamonds in the light. If the Iraqis hadn't invaded their country Amani's and Talal's wedding would have taken place in a few days. Danah's hand reached for her sister's. A tear silently fell from Amani's eye at the touch of Danah's hand. Poor Amani, Danah squeezed Amani's hand, feeling her sister's pain in her own heart.

At the gate of their Aunt's house, mother begged Aziz to stay with them. "My heart will be on fire if I don't see you in front of my eyes," she pleaded.

"Listen to your mother Aziz," father said. He helped Bimla and Talal get the food boxes out of the trunk.

"Just tonight Yumma," Aziz said. He pulled out the fax machine from the trunk. "I need to take care of things with Talal tonight. Tomorrow I will be back and stay with you, in Sha' Allah."

Amani drew the fax she received that morning out of her pocket and handed it to Aziz. "You'll have to take care of this yourself now," she whispered. She took a few steps to the main door of the house, hesitated, then turned toward Talal. Looking at him affectionately, she softly said, "Would you please take care of yourself?"

Talal didn't answer. He stood in front of Amani and gazed at her silently.

Danah put her arm around Amani's shoulder. "And Talal," she said. "Could you please come and visit us from time to time?"

Talal's handsome face finally smiled. He unexpectedly stretched his hand to shake Danah's hand. "I'm glad you came back," he said.

"Me too." Danah smiled.

He then took Amani's hand and held it for a long moment

without saying a word. Danah wanted to leave them alone but Amani turned around and walked inside the house with her, not looking back.

Aunt Hussah was waiting for their arrival. She hugged Danah tightly. "You are a brave girl Danah," she whispered in her ears. "Al hamdu Lillah for your safety."

"Thank you," Danah said, feeling safe in her great aunt's arms.

"Each one of you can have her own room," Aunt Hussah said to Danah and Amani after showing their parents to their room. "I have these rooms all furnished for my grandchildren and their parents. They haven't used them once yet."

"Do you have a basement?" Amani asked.

"Fortunately I do. The door to it is right in front of the main entrance, in case we need to go there tonight."

"I hope we don't," Danah said, walking behind her aunt. "Let me help you with those."

Khalah Hussah, as everyone in Danah's family called her, was seventy seven. Yet she carried a stack of blankets and pillows with ease.

"No my child, I can do it," she said.

"Have you heard from your family?"

"Not for a month, two weeks, and five days. But they are certainly safe far away from here. They must be more worried about me. But let's not talk about worry."

She placed the stack of sheets on the bed and turned to Danah. She opened her arms wide and gave Danah a tight hug. "Tomorrow is a new day. May Allah make it a better day for all of us."

"Insha' Allah," said Danah. But when Khalah Hussa turned off the lights and shut the door, Danah lay awake in bed wondering if a better day would ever arrive.

CHAPTER EIGHTEEN

August 28, 1990

*E*ARLY IN THE MORNING, Danah sat next to Khalah Hussa on the floor of the living room, and gazed at one of the old black and white photographs her aunt handed her. She pointed at a figure in one of them. "Who is this funny man?"

Khalah Hussa peered at the man Danah pointed at and smiled. "That's my father. And I don't think he's funny. Why is he funny?"

Danah felt embarrassed. "I used the wrong word, not funny, but different. His hair is longer than the other men's, and he's barefoot."

"He was a brilliant man, may Allah have mercy on him," Khalah Hussa said. "Sometimes I think you inherited his fiery spirit."

Danah smiled at her aunt and flipped the picture to the next one. "Allah, who's this beautiful girl?"

"This is Bedr el bedoor, your great grandmother. She was the most beautiful girl of her time."

Danah gazed at the woman in the picture, comparing her

to Amani. "She does look like Amani, don't you think?"

Khalah Hussa nodded. "But she was so unlucky, she died giving birth to her first child."

"Danah! Don't you want to go with me?" Amani stood at the living room entrance. She had already wrapped her black abaya over her head and around her body.

"Where are you going?" Danah asked.

"To a neighbor's house, not far."

Danah sensed that Amani really wanted her to go along. She handed the pictures to her aunt. "I'll change in a minute."

"You don't have to change, just put an abaya over your gown."

Danah raised her eyebrows. "I don't have an abaya."

"Take mine," Khalah Hussa said. "It will be a little short on you, but it'll be fine. "

Outside, Danah asked, "Who are we going to see?"

"Some people mother knows. She talked to them this morning. It seems they need help." Amani adjusted the abaya over her head.

Danah glanced at Amani, her face was so serious it made her heart wince. She followed her sister's steps over the sandy sidewalk. Their footsteps crunched loudly in the empty streets. The heat of the sun slowly penetrated her abaya, and made her skin feel like the hot sand.

A few minutes later, Amani turned into a small street and stopped in front of a house with high adobe walls and a heavy wooden gate. She rang the bell, then looked at Danah with worried eyes. She whispered, "I hope they're not badly hurt."

"Who?" Danah whispered back.

"Their two sons. They…"

The gate opened and a Filipino maid led them toward the

house through a garden where flowers and roses had once flourished. At the door of the living room, Danah's heart sank.

A sound came from within, it brought goose bumps to her skin. At first she couldn't recognize the sound but then she knew: wailing. Women wailing for the dead.

Amani stepped in first. Women and children were sobbing and whimpering out loud. Amani approached a lady in the middle of the room, and crouched next to her. "Strengthen your heart Om Jasem. This is what Allah has willed for us."

"I know my daughter, I know," Om Jasem said.

"Where are your sons?" Amani asked.

Om Jasem pointed to a room in a hallway behind them.

"May I see them? Perhaps I can do something to help."

Om Jasem wiped her tears and looked toward a middle aged woman sitting next to her.

"I'll take her," the woman said, rising to her feet.

Danah followed Amani who seemed to know the woman, calling her by the name of Fatima. In front of a closed door Fatima hesitated. She looked at Danah then to Amani. "Is your sister strong? The young one…"

"What happened to them?" asked Danah, feeling perspiration gather over her forehead and around her lips.

"The Iraqis took them about a week ago. They dragged young Ahmed to their truck and when his brother Jasem tried to get him out they took him as well."

Amani reached over and turned the door knob. A powerful stench overwhelmed them. Danah took a step back and covered her nose with her abaya. The windows and curtains were shut in the dark room. As Danah's eyes adjusted to the light, she saw two emaciated shapes, laying on two separate beds. They didn't look like they were human or alive, more like animals that had been mistreated by cruel kids.

113

"Where is their father?" asked Danah, her eyes frozen on the two bodies.

Fatima, still standing by the door answered. "The poor man's looking for a doctor to come and see his boys."

"Why didn't he take them to the hospital?" Danah asked, choking on her tears. It was the worst sight she'd ever seen. The boys' skin was unnaturally blue. There were black spots all over the young one's face. She began to sob.

Amani took a quick look at the boys and turned toward Danah. She took her by the arm and whispered, "Danah, we didn't come here to cry. Come with me."

She led Danah to the kitchen. Danah wiped her face with her abaya and watched Amani get two glasses and fill them with water from a cooler next to the sink. She grabbed a clean towel and moistened it with water.

Back in the room, Amani approached the smaller shape. She crouched down next to Ahmed's bed and called his name repeatedly. She touched his shoulder. Still there was no response. There were large blood stains all over the boy's dish-dasha.

"I hope he's just unconscious," Amani's voice trembled. She crawled over to the other bed. Gently, she wiped Jasem's face with the moist towel. His eyes opened.

"Danah quick, bring the water! Help me give him some."

Danah held the glass to his lips while Amani tilted up his head. Jasem managed to drink some water before he dropped his head back and moaned.

Danah thought she saw Amani whisper something in Jasem's ear, upon which he got quiet and strained to open his eyes again. He looked at Amani briefly.

"I didn't reveal anything," he said in a rasping voice. "Not a word."

"Sh sh," Amani said. "It's all right now."

"They tortured us continuously for three days. They threatened to kill me and my brother."

"Where did they take you?" Amani asked.

"To the Alarabi Sports Club in Mansuriya. They beat us and electrocuted us while asking us questions."

"What kind of questions?" asked Amani.

"Do you work for the resistance? Do you know any members of the resistance? Do you know where westerners are hiding? Every time we said no to these questions they threw salt and pepper in our eyes. They pulled out our fingernails." He started to lift his limp hand but did not have the strength.

Danah shut her eyes and looked away, she felt faint and sick at heart.

But Jasem went on, "I should have talked, I should have..." he sobbed. "Ahmed, poor Ahmed, he didn't know anything. Yet they hit him with an iron pipe in front of me. They hit him so hard."

His tears flowed to the sides of his face. Amani wiped them with the towel.

"He was crying so bad. He swore he didn't know anything but they didn't believe him. The way they hit him... How could they do that to a sweet young boy like Ahmed?" Jasem gasped for air. "Allah, Allah forgive me for what I did to him. It's my fault."

"You had no choice," said Amani.

"I could have told them something. I could have saved him from the torture he suffered."

Jasem paused for a moment. "They took us both into a small chamber. First they interrogated Ahmed in front of me. When he didn't answer they hit me with an iron pipe. Poor Ahmed, he cringed every time they hit me. Sometimes they beat me on the arms and legs, later on the face. They were trying to get him to talk, but Ahmed knew nothing.

"Then they lit a torch and threatened to burn him in front of my eyes. They waved the fire in front of his face. His eyes looked so big, I could see the fire reflected in them. Then they drew the fire close to his bare chest, I could smell the burns. When he fainted they poured water over him. He woke up every time screaming my name. I should have protected him. He was my little brother, I should have…"

Jasem sobbed bitterly. Danah sobbed also, while Amani tried to calm Jasem down. "You had no choice," she repeated.

"This morning," Jasem continued, "they blindfolded about thirty of us and took us outside. They told us we would all be shot if we didn't talk. Instead someone sang: "ana elkuwaiti, I am Kuwaiti". We heard gun shots. The singing stopped, then after a few moments it resumed faintly. More gun shots. Then silence followed for what seemed like eternity. I didn't feel anything. I stood there for a long time, shaking, until my blindfold was removed. Some of the prisoners were standing, like me. Others were on the ground, in puddles of blood. Ahmed was on the ground…"

For the first time, Danah saw Amani cry uncontrollably. She covered her face with her hands, and wept, her shoulders shook under her abaya. Danah turned away, tried not to look at poor Ahmed's body.

Two men appeared at the door led by Fatima. She touched Amani's shoulder and helped her get up.

Bu Jasem, along with another man, carrying a black medical case, hurried into the room. Amani took Danah's hand and pulled her out of the room.

"Let's say goodbye to Om Jasem." Amani wiped her face and pulled her abaya over her head.

The woman hugged Amani and Danah. She thanked them for their visit, and prayed that God would keep the Iraqis away from them and their loved ones.

"Ameen," Amani said, her eyes filling with tears again. Without uttering a word they returned to Khalah Hussa's house. Amani went straight to the phone and made a call.

Danah remained quiet the rest of the morning. She was shocked and angered at what was happening to her country-men. Imprisoned for what? Tortured for what? Killed for what? There were no reasons to justify those crimes. None.

Rage and resentment grew inside her by the second. She remembered Bu Salem and Salem, their neighbors in Khaledeya, who were taken by the Iraqis. She imagined them being tortured and killed. She couldn't stop crying at that thought. How long was this going to go on? How long? Were they going to spend the rest of their lives captives in their own country? Were they going to be Iraqis, never Kuwaitis, as that man in Washington had told her over the phone?

Danah left her room and marched down to Amani's. As usual these days, Amani was reading letters that she immediately put away when Danah approached.

"Amani!" Danah said standing at the foot of Amani's bed. "I want do something."

"What do you mean?"

"I'm so angry I have to do something. I can't just hide in the house while those poor young men get tortured and killed."

Amani gazed at Danah as if she'd seen her for the first time. She lowered her voice. "There is a group of women who help the resistance."

"I want to join them."

Amani looked over Danah's shoulders at the door and

whispered, "The problem is mother, she would not let you leave the house. She's so worried."

"So is father."

Amani lowered her voice again. "There is a meeting in Kaifan tonight that I want to go to, but how?"

"We can walk there," Danah whispered back.

"It's too far."

"That's true, I wish we had bicycles."

Amani smiled. "But I can't ride, remember? I need Julie to teach me."

"I'll teach you."

"Well, we don't have bicycles anyway. Do you really think we can walk in this heat?"

"What time is the meeting?"

"Seven."

Danah thought for a second. "If the meeting is over at eight, by the time we walk back it will be about ten. Mother will be running down the streets screaming our names."

Amani nodded deep in thought. "Let me see what I can do." Then she looked Danah in the eye. "Are you serious about wanting to work with the resistance?"

"Yes, of course I'm serious," Danah said, remembering her friend Zainah at the Saudi camp and her father Bu Thamer. God, she missed them so much, she would give anything to see them again.

Amani checked the time on her wrist watch. "I have to make a phone call. I'll let you know if we can do something about the meeting tonight."

In the afternoon, right after the call for prayers, Amani walked into Danah's room and closed the door behind her.

"Are we going?" Danah asked anxiously.

"Ssh," Amani said, placing her forefinger over her lips. She

118

sat on the floor next to Danah who was looking at some scraps of cloth.

"You are going," she whispered in Danah's ear.

Danah raised her eyebrows. "Alone? How?"

"Do you remember the woman I talked to at Om Jasem's house this morning?"

Danah nodded. "Fatima."

"She said she's got a bicycle for you to go to Kaifan."

Danah's eyes opened wide.

"Wear the same clothes you wore when you rode Thamer's bike, so people will think you're a boy."

"Can't you go with me?"

"I wish, I really wish I could, but we'd have to walk, and that would take a long time. Then mother would find out and you know the rest of the story. But if you put the abaya over your jeans when we leave the house, we'll tell mother we're going to see how Om Jasem's sons are doing."

When Danah didn't object, Amani continued, "We'll go to Fatima's house, next door to Om Jasem's. She'll have the bike ready for you and an envelope which we need you to deliver to somebody at the meeting."

"Then?"

"Then get back. You don't have to stay for the meeting. I'll be waiting for you at Fatima's house with your abaya and we'll walk back here together."

Danah smiled with excitement. "As if nothing happened."

"As if nothing happened," Amani repeated, but not so excitedly.

Danah stood up. "I'm ready, let's go."

"I told Fatima we'd be at her house at six."

Danah ignored the fear that grew steadily inside her, and got ready for her mission. She pinned her hair back, wore blue jeans and a short sleeved shirt. She found a small backpack in one of the chest drawers. She would carry a bottle of water and whatever they wanted her to deliver to the meeting.

At fifteen minutes to six, Amani came to her room holding an abaya in her hand. "Are you ready?" she asked Danah nervously.

Danah put the Disney World cap inside the backpack, which she slipped onto her back. She took the abaya from Amani, held it over her head, and wrapped it around her shoulders.

"Now I'm ready," she said, swallowing hard. Her throat already dry.

"I told mother we're going to Om Jasem's house. So let's just go."

The two girls slipped quietly out the front door and hurried toward the gate.

"Where are you going?"

Danah and Amani jerked around at the unexpected question. It was Aziz with father. They had just returned from the mosque.

"We're going to see if Om Jasem needs anything," Amani answered.

"Don't stay out late, Zain?" father said, concern in his voice.

"Zain Yuba," Amani said.

Danah bit her lower lip nervously. She wanted to fly out of the house before Aziz's suspicious eyes discovered their secret. But Amani casually put her arm around her shoulders, calming her down.

At Fatima's house, they stopped and looked at each other. Danah smiled.

"I'm endangering your life, Danah," Amani said, her eyes filling with tears. "Don't do it, let's go back." She pulled Danah by the arm.

"No," Danah said. "I want to do it, I want to help."

The door opened. Fatima pointed to the bicycle leaning on the wall behind the gate. In her hand she held a large brown envelope.

"I didn't write the address, you have to memorize it."

Danah gave Amani her abaya while she listened carefully to Fatima's instructions. She took the envelope and felt it with her fingers. It was stuffed with paper. Placing it in her pack, she got ready to mount the bike as Fatima opened the gate.

"It's better not to know what's inside, otherwise you might be nervous," Fatima was saying.

"Danah," Amani's voice broke while she hugged her tightly. "Please be careful. If you think it's too dangerous to keep going, just come back."

Danah kept a smile on her face until she rode out of the women's sight. Once she was alone she concentrated on how to take the shortest way to Kaifan. She should go through Yarmouk, Khaledeya and then Kaifan. Remembering Bu Thamer's advice, Danah took side roads and streets. If it wasn't for the fear of being caught, she would have enjoyed the ride. The streets were unnaturally quiet. The sun had slipped down, leaving only hazy light on the western horizon. But even at ten minutes to seven in the evening, it was scorching hot.

Danah's worries returned once she rode into Kaifan district. The lights of the supermarket were lit and there were more people about than she had encountered in Yarmouk or Khaledeya. Again she avoided the main streets until somehow, she found herself in front of the house she was looking for.

An old Kuwaiti man was sitting in front of the gate. She leaned the bike on the trunk of a palm tree. Danah recited the secret code carefully. The man led her inside the house. A

121

group of women with tiny babies in their laps sat in a circle on the floor of the living room.

"Salam Alaikum," Danah said.

"Alaikum al-salam," the women answered in unison.

"I need to see Asrar," Danah said to one of them.

"She's not here yet." The woman rocked a baby in her lap. "But in sha' Allah, she'll be here soon."

Another woman noticed that Danah was nervous. "You want to hold this baby?" she said to Danah with a smile. "Isn't she so sweet?"

Danah took the baby in her arms. She looked like an angel with big blue eyes.

"These babies," the woman explained, "were thrown out of their incubators by the Iraqi soldiers when they stormed the hospital during the first week of the invasion. The Iraqis took the incubators to Iraq and left those babies helpless without care. Some of them were prematurely born and needed care."

"Where are their parents?" Danah asked bewildered.

The woman shrugged. "God only knows. They either left Kuwait without being able to get their babies, or they were killed by the Iraqi soldiers."

Danah gazed at the blue eyed baby and wondered what happened to her parents. "So how did you bring the babies here?"

"Some of the nurses that worked in the hospital took the babies and asked around for help. We volunteered to take care of them with the help of a Kuwaiti female doctor."

A commotion sounded outside which made the woman stop talking. Gun shots could be heard in the distance along with car horns and screeching tires.

A woman ran outside while the other women stared at

122

each other. As if mesmerized, they began singing: An elkuwaiti, I am the Kuwaiti.

Five minutes later, a young woman, in her early thirties, barged in with a smile on her face.

"What is it Asrar?" everybody said.

"Oh, I just drove through those idiots' checkpoint without stopping." She laughed. "But don't worry, I lost them. Where is Danah?"

Danah stood up facing Asrar.

"Do you have something for me?"

Nodding, Danah pulled the envelope out of her backpack and handed it to her.

"There is someone outside who wants to see you," she whispered in Danah's ear. "Thank you Danah, God bless you."

"And you," Danah said, full of admiration for the brave young woman.

Danah ran outside. Next to her bicycle stood a tall bearded young man. He was holding a brown bag in his hand. In spite of his nervousness, he smiled a big smile when he saw her.

"Danah, you have to leave right this minute."

Danah stared at the young man who looked familiar but she couldn't recognize him. When he asked her to please give the brown bag to Amani, she yelled, "Talal! I couldn't recognize you because of the beard."

He smiled again. "Please leave now Danah, don't waste any time. And be safe."

He opened the gate for her. Danah rode through slowly and said, "Talal you should visit us soon." She looked up. Her eyes met his big beautiful eyes, and her heart sank. She had never seen sadder eyes in her life. Talal didn't answer, he just nodded while holding the gate open for her.

Danah pedaled away apprehensively. It was getting dark,

and the sound of machine guns and explosions in the distance was unsettling. Talal's sad eyes followed her all the way back, like a big wave in a dark sea, warning of an approaching storm.

Safe inside Fatima's house she hugged Amani for a long time.

"Thank God you're back," said Amani over and over.

"I have something for you from Talal," Danah whispered in her sister's ear.

"Did you see Asrar?" Fatima asked.

"Yes and she took the envelope," Danah said. "What was in it?"

"Strategic maps, and lots of money from our government in exile," Fatima answered. "The money is to help the women take care of the babies you saw, and to bribe the Iraqis to release prisoners."

Amani grabbed Danah's hand. "So you see Danah, you helped save many lives tonight."

On their way back to Khalah Hussa's house, Amani asked Danah to tell her everything in the minutest details. Danah made sure she finished her story right at the gate of their aunt's house.

Inside Danah's room, Amani locked the door and waited for the bag that Talal sent. From the bag, Amani pulled out a cloth with four colors: black, white, green, and red. It was the Kuwaiti flag. A letter, hidden inside the flag, fell to the floor. Danah picked it up and gave it to Amani.

Amani hugged the flag to her heart, and clutched the letter in her hand. Danah knew that it was time for her to exit, and leave her sister alone with a few happy thoughts.

CHAPTER NINETEEN

September 5, 1990

Dear Julie,

Today was supposed to be Amani's wedding day. If Saddam hadn't invaded our country, you would be here and we would be celebrating the occasion, wearing beautiful clothes, listening to beautiful music.

Instead, we are all wearing the same clothes we wore yesterday, listening to gun shots and the sound of explosions. Amani hasn't left her room all morning, neither has mother. They both can't stop crying.

We are staying at Khalah Hussah's house. We left our house in Khaledeya because it was too dangerous and too close to the Iraqi soldiers. Even here, we still see them occasionally. They come over sometimes to ask for water. Khalah Hussah gives them some. She is a great lady and fun to be with. When everyone in my family is busy doing something I sit next to her in the living room and ask her to tell me stories about her childhood. She is fascinating, I hope you'll get to meet her one day.

Yesterday I asked her why Saddam invaded our country. She said, "It is mainly ignorance and greed. No one who's educated and can think would do what he did." Then she said, "Ignorant people love power, and he wanted to take over our oil and then move to Saudi Arabia and take their oil and on to the Emirates. That way he would control more than half of the world's oil. He would then manipulate the whole world with the power of oil. Just imagine what the world would be like at that point!" That's what Khalah Hussah said, she is so smart.

We listen to the radio almost all the time, especially the Voice of America. It's great hearing that the world has not forgotten us. We're hoping that Saddam will leave Kuwait peacefully so war will not be necessary.

Julie, I want to thank you again for the cap you gave me, it saved my life and Aziz's, my brother. One day, I will tell you the story in detail.

I miss you and Uncle Faisal a great deal. I haven't had the chance to finish **Les Miserables** but I will resume reading again soon. I have plenty of time to read now.

I will write you from time to time until I find someone who can mail my letters to you so you will be assured of our safety. Thank you again for your hospitality. Give my love to my uncle.

Love, Danah

October 7, 1990

Dear Julie,

Something horrible happened last week, the Iraqis took Talal! They found out that he was working for the resistance, came to his house, dragged him out in front of his family, pushed him in their truck and took him away. Julie, I'm so sad, why do these things happen? Why?

Amani almost lost her mind when she heard the news. She is better now but she will not leave her room or talk to anyone. I stay by her side almost all the time and feel her grief and sorrow. I just can't believe these things are happening to us. I wish I appreciated our life before this happened.

Mother now watches Aziz like an eagle protecting her chicks. She won't let him leave the house for a minute. I don't blame her. I worry about him too, but I try not to think about it all the time.

A week ago the Iraqis imposed a curfew. We cannot go out in the streets between 11 p.m. and 7 a.m. The Kuwaiti resistance during that time blew up Iraqi tanks and military centers. But they are paying dearly for those actions, they're giving up their lives. Julie, everyday we hear about young innocent Kuwaiti men getting tortured and killed by the Iraqi soldiers. I just don't want to talk about it otherwise my heart will break into pieces. Do you think they'll spare Talal's life?

I'm sorry I'm telling you sad news but I need to talk to someone because everyone here suddenly got silent.

Danah

127

December 2, 1990

Dear Julie,

Last month was very difficult for us. Amani got very ill and we needed to take her to the hospital, but the Iraqis only allow wounded Iraqi soldiers there. Fortunately one of our neighbors told us about a female relative of hers who is a doctor. We called her and she came over and stayed with Amani for two days. After Amani got better mother fell ill with high blood pressure. The doctor gave her the last pills she had for lowering blood pressure. She said many old Kuwaitis are suffering from high blood pressure these days, but my mother is not very old.

Ten days ago the Iraqis lifted the curfew. They are announcing that life is back to normal now in Kuwait. What a lie, nothing is normal here any more.

A week ago, Amani, myself and a group of other neighbors began walking around the neighborhood and checking on families who are in need of food or other help. We decided to start our own bakery in one of the neighbor's houses because all bakeries are closed now. We want to give bread to those who need it. It feels good to help other people.

We listen to the news all the time and feel grateful that the whole world is on our side. We still hope that Saddam will leave without a war. How can he think he will win when the most advanced countries are sending their armies to help us?

However, we are getting ready in case a war begins. We are storing some food, although there isn't much, in the basement along with water, a radio, blankets, and candles. Julie, I'm scared of war.

Danah

December 20, 1990

Oh Julie,

The pain in my heart is indescribable. We are living a nightmare. Something we never dreamed of happened. They killed him. They stopped his heart from beating. They killed Talal. Young Talal, brave Talal is gone. I keep hoping, praying that it's only a nightmare, that I will wake up and find out it's not true.

Sorry about the spots on the paper, I couldn't stop my tears from falling since it happened last week. Julie, they dragged poor Talal alive from their truck and then shot him dead right in front of his parents. Right in front of their eyes. I just can't believe it. To just kill someone like that!

What kind of behavior is that? What kind of human beings could do such a thing? Don't they have hearts?

Oh Julie, I'm so so sad I could die. When I think of his mother and father I get sick to my stomach. And poor poor Amani, she has lost her mind.

The horrors just don't stop. Yesterday I heard about a young Kuwaiti woman whom I met briefly some time ago and admired immensely. Her name was Asrar. The Iraqis arrested her and tortured her. After they killed her, they left her body wrapped in a blanket in front of her parents' house.

How we're going to live on through this nightmare, I don't know. I don't think I'll ever be happy again.

Danah

January 10, 1991

Dear Julie,

Did you celebrate New Year's eve? I wish you did although I have a feeling you didn't. How is Uncle Faisal?

Last night we all gathered around a coal fire in the living room with some gasoline torches and a transistor radio. We don't have electricity anymore. No phones either, the Iraqis cut off all lines. The house is freezing now that we're without heat.

Two days ago, we were able to go out to visit some relatives who lived close to downtown. Father drove Aziz's car while we all held our breath every time the Iraqi soldiers stopped us at a check point, and there were many of them. They asked to see father's driver's license and ID card. They looked at us closely one by one, and then asked to search our trunk.

Julie, you won't believe what happened to our beautiful city. It is totally ruined and deserted. Destruction everywhere. Buildings burnt and looted. It's worse than a nightmare.

Our New Year's wish is that we will be free in 1991.

We feel hopeful every time we hear your president, President Bush, on the radio. He's telling Saddam all the things that we wish we could tell him. God bless President Bush and the American people.

Danah

CHAPTER TWENTY

January 17, 1991

DANAH WAS DEEP ASLEEP when she became aware of her mother calling her name. Finally she opened her eyes but mother was not in the basement. It was very dark and cold. She could hear noises coming from upstairs as well as from outside the house.

Danah wrapped herself in a blanket and groped her way in the dark toward the faint light that came from the first floor. "What's going on?" she asked, hoping someone would answer her.

Upstairs, her family, including Khalah Hussah, gathered around a gasoline light on the floor, and listened intently to a transistor radio. The noises outside became louder, Danah could feel the sound vibrations through her body. She sat next to the light and looked at her wristwatch. It was 2:00 a.m.

Aziz who held the radio in his hands looked at her and smiled. "Congratulations," he said. "The war began."

Danah felt a cold shiver pierce through her heart, her mind in a state of confusion. The two words 'congratulations' and 'war' just did not make sense together. She moved her eyes from face to face. Her father's face looked serious. Her mother's face looked anxious, while hope filled Amani's face. Her aunt's looked serene and reflective.

The man on the radio, an Arab announcer, repeatedly described how the Allied forces began bombing Baghdad and the Iraqis' military centers in Kuwait. The sound of planes and explosions could be heard in the radio and outside.

Suddenly Danah began weeping. She couldn't control herself even though they all expected this to happen since the fifteenth of January, when President Bush gave Saddam a deadline to leave Kuwait. Since then Kuwaitis inside Kuwait were told by the government in exile through radio broadcasts to stay in shelters and basements, and prepare for war conditions. Still Danah couldn't believe it would happen. But now it had, war had begun, and more people would die for the actions of one man. Why should a horrible thing like that happen? Why? Danah cried even more.

"What is it?" Amani asked gently touching her shoulder.

"You should be happy instead of crying," Aziz said. "This is the best news since August second, this is what we've been waiting for."

"I hate war," Danah sobbed.

"That's the only way we will be freed," Aziz said over the voice of the radio announcer.

"But how about the people who will be killed during the war?" Danah said between sobs.

No one answered her question except the roar of planes above their heads in the sky outside. Her family remained quiet. Danah felt embarrassed adding to their grief. She swallowed her sorrow and forced herself to calm down. She stared at the transistor radio, finding the news that came from it incomprehensible.

Finally, her father's voice came sounding strange and far, as if coming from a different person. "This is how it all began. Exactly the same, Thursday morning, we woke up to the same noise. Let the people who rejoiced over our misery taste the same pain."

Danah wiped her tears and looked up at him. "I'm sorry Yuba." She touched his arm, he was shaking.

"I'm going outside to watch," Aziz said standing up.

"No!" Danah's mother screamed. "It's dangerous. Tell him not to," she said to her husband.

"Aziz listen to your mother," father said faintly. But Aziz had already left the living room.

Danah moved closer to Khalah Hussah and hugged her. Her aunt put her arms around her and patted her on the shoulder. "Let's pray for those brave people fighting for us," she whispered in Danah's ears.

Danah closed her eyes feeling the salty tears in the corners of her lips. She prayed silently to God to save everybody and everyone helping to free her country.

———◆———

Four weeks went slowly by while the Allied forces pounded the Iraqi military establishment in Iraq and Kuwait by air. During those weeks Danah and her family grew anxious wanting to see all the Iraqi forces leave their country. Mother and Aziz argued a great deal. Aziz, like so many young men, encouraged by the air strikes on the Iraqis, wanted to go out and fight. But mother would not hear of it. She would not let him out of her sight, she would even follow him whenever he walked out to the street.

It was funny, Danah thought, but she didn't blame her mother. Many Kuwaitis who did what Aziz wanted to do were killed by the Iraqis who were frightened now and easily threatened by any activity. The Iraqi soldiers began rounding up hundreds of young Kuwaiti men as hostages and as shields against the air strikes and the expected ground war.

And finally the day most Kuwaitis had dreamed of arrived. Ground war began on the afternoon of February 24th. Aziz and his father climbed to the roof of the house and watched clouds of helicopters manned by the Allied forces hover over Kuwait City. That was how the ground war started.

The very next day, the 25th, Iraqi troops began withdrawing. Hundreds of military vehicles moved in long lines on the highway north back toward Iraq.

"That was an incredible sight," Aziz said later in the basement. A big smile formed on his face, bringing back the happy look which had vanished since Danah saw him after the invasion. "I wish I could follow them and make sure they're going the right way."

"No you cannot," mother said. She was holding the radio in her hand, her dark tired face showing some life in it. "Listen to what they're saying." She turned up the volume.

The Kuwaiti broadcaster from a station in Saudi Arabia implored all people in Kuwait to stay in their houses and not leave until the Allied troops 'purged' Kuwait of the 'invaders'. He excitedly reported that the Kuwaiti island of Failaka had already been liberated and the Kuwaiti flag hoisted up again.

"Yeah!" Danah, and Aziz cheered at the same time.

Amani hugged Khalah Hussah and together they wept. "I wish Talal were alive to hear this," Amani sobbed, while Khalah Hussah patted her shoulder.

"Mabrook, congratulations, Yumma." Danah hugged her mother.

"I'm going to talk with the neighbors," Father said.

"I'm going with you." Aziz followed him while mother's eyes followed them silently.

"It's all right Yumma," Danah said. "He's with father, and father won't go far."

"Shinoo? What's going on?" Bimla asked.

Danah explained that the Kuwaiti island of Failaka had just been liberated, which meant that freedom was getting close. Bimla happily clapped her hands and danced.

Freedom actually came much sooner than anyone of them thought. Three days later President Bush announced: "The war is over. Kuwait is liberated. The Iraqi army is defeated."

To those simple beautiful words, Danah, her parents, Aziz and Amani wept tears of joy and happiness. They were sitting in the living room listening to President Bush's speech announcing cease fire, 100 hours after the beginning of the ground war.

"Who wants to celebrate?" Aziz announced picking up his car keys from the coffee table.

"I do," Khalah Hussah exclaimed hopping up. The others looked at each other and laughed.

"We all do of course," Danah said.

Jammed in Aziz's car, Danah's family along with Bimla drove out of Cordoba toward Kuwait City. The streets were crowded with cars and people walking and driving, honking and waving at each other. Kuwaiti flags fluttered everywhere, flags which had brought the death penalty to those found carrying them during the last seven months of the Iraqi occupation.

It was a cold gray day. Dark clouds of smoke filled the sky coming from the south where 500 Kuwaiti oil fields, ignited by the Iraqi soldiers, burnt with raging fires. The city was in ruins. Yet in the middle of it all, Kuwaitis celebrated. They danced and sang and thanked the troops who had miraculously liberated their country.

CHAPTER TWENTY ONE

Dear Julie,

Two days ago I witnessed the happiest day of my life. We are free, Kuwait is free, finally free. I cannot describe my feelings, but I'm sure you understand. I can imagine Uncle Faisal's happy face now, and can hear his unique way of laughing, the one I love so much.

Everyone here is so ecstatic. (I just looked up this word in the Thesaurus under happy. It sounded like the best one to describe my feelings). Except for poor Amani of course. Her grief is immense, and no one can blame her. Talal worked so hard for this day, but he never got to see it. The Iraqi soldiers took his young life away, but we will never forget him, and those who died to free our country.

We are still staying at Khalah Hussah's house. I think we will stay here until electricity and water are restored. She is the neatest lady. The other day when we went downtown to celebrate she grabbed a shy young American soldier and kissed him on the cheek. We are so thankful to the half million American personnel who participated in liberating our country, to the American people, and President Bush, our

137

hero. His pictures are displayed everywhere in our streets and houses.

We are also grateful to the Saudis, Egyptians, Emiratis, and Syrians who joined the Allied forces and fought against the Iraqi Army. The British, French, Canadians, and so many other nationalities deserve our thanks and gratitude. Without them we couldn't have been freed. I wish Saddam listened to President Bush when he said, "It's the whole world against Saddam."

By the way, I finished reading Les Miserables. Thank you so much for giving it to me. During the invasion, I thought of us Kuwaitis as the Miserables. Now I think the Iraqi people are the miserable ones until they too are freed from Saddam's tyranny.

Julie, there are so many things to be done now in my country. I would like to help clean and rebuild our university and schools. Myself and some of my girlfriends, especially those I met during the invasion, want to form a group to help restore what the Iraqi soldiers destroyed. One of those places is the Zoo, which needs a great deal of attention now.

For those reasons I don't think I can visit you and Uncle Faisal this summer. Disney World has to wait, until my country is recovered and rebuilt the way it used to be, the pearl of the Gulf. Please say 'In Sha' Allah', you say it so well!

> *Love,*
> *Danah*
> *February 26, 1991*